Queen of Diamonds

"*Queen of Diamonds* is the second collaboration between Frank Zafiro and Jim Wilsky and it's a partnership that runs like a well-oiled machine...I've read a lot of books set in Las Vegas, but there are very few I have enjoyed more."

—Chris Leek, independent reviewer

"Zafiro and Wilsky manage to both frustrate some expectations readers may have and bring everything to a satisfying conclusion."

—Brian Triplett, independent reviewer

Acclaim for the Ania Series

"Dark and nasty good. I haven't had this much fun reading about two brothers since Cain and Abel."

—Brad Parks, award-winning author of the Carter Ross Series

"A hell of a good story told by a pair of aces, guaranteed to jump-start your heart from the very first word. Add this to your reading list for sure!"

—Shane Gericke, bestselling author of *Torn Apart*

"Zafiro and Wilsky have teamed up to deliver a stunning punch to the head with *Blood on Blood*. Tightly plotted and perfectly executed. If you like your fiction boiled hard, don't pass this one up."

—Al Leverone, author of *The Lonely Mile*

"...a straight shot of raw, fiery, undiluted noir. Dangerous dudes and even more dangerous dames conspire, connive, and collide with deadly results in a bare-bones, no-nonsense thriller that takes no prisoners. A definite must-read for those who take their crime fiction strong and dark."
—JD Rhoades, author of the Jack Keller series

"*Blood on Blood* is one helluva great read."
—Bill Cameron, author of *County Line*

"*Blood on Blood* brings more than enough grit to keep you happily flipping through its nasty, nasty pages."
—Todd "Big Daddy Thug" Robinson, author of *Dirty Words* and *The Hard Bounce*

"If you like it mean and menacing, down and dirty, *Blood on Blood* is right up your dark alley."
—Earl Staggs, Derringer Award-winning author

"*Blood on Blood* is an intense and truly addictive thriller that captures you immediately and holds you bound until the last page."
—Julia Madeleine, author of *The Truth About Scarlet Rose*

"Just when you thought you'd seen and re-seen every possible crime plot, along comes *Blood on Blood*. Zafiro and Wilsky have put together a fast-moving, authentic thriller, complete with witty dialogue and characters who seem real enough to touch. A beautifully written book, with stunning plot twists throughout. You'll love it!"
—John M. Floyd, award-winning author

QUEEN OF DIAMONDS

ALSO BY FRANK ZAFIRO AND JIM WILSKY

Blood on Blood (#1)
Closing the Circle (#3)
Harbinger (prequel)

ALSO BY JIM WILSKY

Sort 'Em Out Later (*)

ALSO BY FRANK ZAFIRO

River City Series

Under a Raging Moon
Heroes Often Fail
Beneath a Weeping Sky
And Every Man Has to Die

The Menace of the Years
Place of Wrath and Tears
Dirty Little Town (*)

Stefan Kopriva Mysteries

Waist Deep
Lovely, Dark, and Deep

Friends of the Departed

Bricks & Cam Jobs (with Eric Beetner)

The Backlist
The Short List

The Getaway List

With Lawrence Kelter

The Last Collar
No Dibs on Murder (*)

Fallen City

With Colin Conway

Some Degree of Murder
Never the Crime
Code Four

Charlie-316
Badge Heavy

SpoCompton Series

At Their Own Game
In the Cut

Love's Laughter (*)
Live and Die This Way (*)

Other Novels

The Ride-Along (*)
The Last Horseman
At This Point in My Life
Some Degree of Murder (w/ Colin Conway

Chisolm's Debt
The Trade Off (w/ Bonnie Paulson)
An Unlikely Phoenix

(*) – Coming Soon

FRANK ZAFIRO
JIM WILSKY

QUEEN OF DIAMONDS
THE ANIA SERIES

Copyright © 2013 by Frank Zafiro and Jim J. Wilsky
Down & Out Books Edition: June 2018
Code 4 Press edition 2021

All rights reserved. No part of the book may be reproduced in any form or by any electronic or mechanical means, including information storage and retrieval systems, without permission in writing from the publisher, except by a reviewer who may quote brief passages in a review.

Code 4 Press, an imprint of Frank Zafiro, LLC

The characters and events in this book are fictitious. Any similarity to real persons, living or dead, is coincidental and not intended by the author.

Cover design by Zach McCain

ISBN: 9781484842744

*For Brad Hallock,
the friend who has stuck with me for the
last twenty years, flush or bust.*
—Frank

*To my family and friends who provide never-ending
support, sacrifice and encouragement.*
—Jim

I long ago came to the conclusion that all life is six to five against.
—Damon Runyon

ONE
Ania

The highway sign gave her a choice, and Ania always believed in choices.

Left two lanes for L.A. and then maybe even north to San Francisco.

Right two lanes heading straight into Las Vegas.

While she knew she was going on to California, she still liked the idea of having an option.

She had a while to think about that.

Casting a quick glance over to the black leather computer bag on the passenger seat, she patted it softly then did a happy little tap with her fingers on the steering wheel. It was a small purchase she had made at a Best Buy back in Denver. A nice satchel, all business, shoulder strap, buckles and zippers, the whole bit.

Looking up into the rearview mirror, she curled a loose strand of luxurious hair behind her ear and studied herself. She was happy with this color, thanks to Lyla's Boutique in trendy Vail. Different than her old color, but still a blonde. Her new dark green contacts weren't bad either. She tried a few quick looks. Smiling big now, then trying a tight thin smile but working the dimples a little.

She pushed the ultra-modern glasses up a little higher with a perfectly manicured finger. The sleek, charcoal-colored frames held nothing but clear glass, but it sure helped the look. She frowned, then arched one eyebrow up as if questioning something, then gave the butter-melting smile again. A natural born actress.

Finding the right disc in the console, she slid it in and turned it up. The trip through Iowa, Nebraska, Colorado, and Utah had been purposely chosen over driving south first to Dallas and then cutting over and down to L.A. Just in case she was followed coming out of Chicago. Just in case. Not that she had really expected that, but hey.

Going this Interstate 80 West route, she would be able to see somebody coming a mile away, literally. Much lighter traffic this way, fewer people and even fewer cops. In general, less everything. Unfortunately, that meant less to do and see on the way too, but Bob Seger had kept her company. Despite her young age, she had always liked the older rock guys. There were no better road songs than Seger's.

Plus, the trip hadn't been a complete bore. Two nights ago, while going through Lincoln, Nebraska of all places, she stopped for a drink on a whim. Met a guy who looked just like Brad Pitt and as it ended up probably better than him in bed. He was a graduate student at the University of Nebraska.

The bar was on the edge of campus, not unlike a few at DePaul she used to hit back in Chicago. Wet tables, loud music, lots of shots, and a lot of fun. No bad stuff, no crimes committed, just living life without a care in the world. She'd left him sleeping it off with a stupid smile still on his face. For the life of her, she couldn't remember his name. Better that way.

Her eyes went back to her business bag, and she thought about how long the two hundred thousand in there might last. She wouldn't be crazy with it, but there would be expenses. It was hard-earned cash, not to be pissed away, at least as she figured it. Hell, that was the way her daddy taught her to earn a living and damned if she wasn't good at it.

No doubt, this haul would keep her off the grift for a while. The ice hidden in her trunk, on the other hand, that would need some additional labor to turn into cash. Big cash though, it would be worth the effort. That was the real deal here. Those rocks were her Super Bowl, the lottery ticket that finally hit. This would be no back-alley deal.

She would just have to see how this rolled. Most importantly, she wouldn't push anything or try to force something. There was plenty of time. Slow and easy is how she would play this. *Let things happen in front of you, not behind you.* One of her dad's favorite sayings.

Ania smiled. It certainly wasn't anything that she couldn't handle. There were men who could help her get this done, and if there was one thing she was best at, it was getting men to do what she wanted them to.

She knew a guy in San Francisco. Sort of. Los Angeles, she didn't know anyone, but you couldn't go five feet without meeting the right kind of man in that city. So, either way...but probably L.A. Maybe.

Ania changed lanes without signaling and then accelerated into the interchange that took her to Las Vegas. She did it without thinking, but as soon as she took the wide turn on the freeway and straightened the wheel, it felt good. It felt right.

Sin City. Never been here.

Seger was singing about turning the page and she turned it up even louder.

She could have some quick fun and maybe even get some serious business done too. There was certainly big money here but maybe not the right kind for the ice. Never know.

Ania cruised slowly down South Las Vegas Boulevard and tried not to gawk. The big places she had always heard of floated and glittered by. Caesars, the MGM Grand, the Mandarin, Luxor, Mandalay Bay, Bellagio, and on and on. A light show like she'd never seen.

She wasn't going to mess around here and stay somewhere just off the strip. Fuck that. She was going all in, as they say here. Just for a couple of days, but hey. Turning around in a parking lot, she came back for another pass and picked the hotel just like the decision to stop here in Vegas. Bang.

She pulled in, and as she approached, going past huge water fountains and seeing the sheer size of this illuminated monster, she knew it was going to be good. She prepped as she slowly drove up.

The Magnum. Celebrating its first anniversary, the sign said. "Holy shit," she muttered as she pulled to a stop. She didn't have her glasses on anymore—didn't fit the occasion. She gave her hair a little shake so it wasn't so perfect and undid one more button on the blouse. She put on her best "what's the big fucking deal?" face as a valet attendant helped her out of the car. She had two small roller bags in the trunk and her satchel, which was already over her shoulder.

"Hold on, I need my purse from one of the bags." She smiled at him after opening the trunk herself.

"Of course, ma'am. Welcome to the Magnum. Is this your first time in Vegas?"

He was her age, probably twenty-four or so, but just goofy as hell. That's okay, though. Not everyone can look like Brad Pitt, and goofus here might just be helpful in some way, you never know.

"No, Will. No, it's not," she said. She liked name-tags for just this reason. He didn't even catch onto how she knew that right away. He was too busy trying to think of something cool and clever to say next. She threw her hair over a shoulder, put her purse inside the bigger bag, and then dangled the keys to him on one finger. "Be careful with the car, okay?"

"Oh yes, yes I will."

Ania stood and waited, smiling her trademark smile at him. She wore jeans that looked painted on, nice heels, and had one hand on her hip.

He blinked twice and smiled back at her.

"Will?" She smiled that smile and cocked her head a little to one side.

"Oh...Uhm, I will, wait, I mean okay. I'm, I'm really sorry." He waved to bellman at the curb and turned back to her. "Michael will help you with your bags, while I do you-rrr car." Red-faced, he waved even harder for Michael.

The lobby took her breath away, but her expression remained flat, one of those "been here done this" looks. Approaching the front desk, she swore to herself, two days, two nights and that's it. No more.

The guy at the desk was efficient and quick. She was lucky. Not only did she get one of the last rooms available, she got upgraded to a suite.

Eyes are everywhere in a casino, and she happened to look up and right into a camera while waiting for him to get her room card. She casually, but at the same time, quickly looked down in her purse, as if she was looking for something. Overreaction? No doubt about it, she thought to herself. She just didn't need to be staring straight up at them. Any cameras, especially security cameras, were just never a good thing. Never.

"Your suite will be on the tenth floor."

"Actually, one of your regular rooms will be fine. I'm only here for two nights." She smiled and got her purse out. *God knows what a suite would cost here.*

"We had a cancellation from one of the top players who just got eliminated. Please, enjoy it, Miss Kozak. The upgrade is on me." The desk clerk smiled at her.

"Top players?"

"The World Championship of Poker. It's being held right here at the Magnum. You're just in time for the final round."

He took out a map of the property and pointed to restaurants, shops, several pools, massage stations, the casino, and nightclub. There was everything a person could possibly think of or want, and all of it was available twenty-four hours a day.

"Thanks so much," she smiled with a heavy sigh, "but all I want right now is a steamy hot bath, a big fluffy robe, and room service."

"We can certainly take care of that right away." He grinned, raised a hand, and waved for someone to help her with her two small bags.

A girl could get used to this, she thought as the elevator whispered her up to a little slice of heaven.

TWO
Cord

I've always been a coffee drinker, and this morning has been no different. From the large silver carafe, I pour my third big cup of this special dark roast from Morocco or some damn place. It's only around eight thirty or so.

Not a cloud in the morning sky, and as I look down at the cars and people, spectacular casinos and hotels are everywhere you look. All that glitz and glamour, but I realize how much I've grown to hate this damn place after just a few days. Vegas is wild and fun, but you can't stay here very long. Or I can't anyway. Soon as this little hoop tee doo is over, and I've done all the right things for the WPA as last years' champ, I'm gone. Besides, I'll have the Atlantic City tournament in two weeks and the Champions circuit starting in New Orleans. Both of those are kickass.

I look away from the wall of windows and walk to the small living room area of the suite. There ain't much left to pick at on the service cart they brought up earlier besides one last piece of bacon. I look at it for a second and then down it like I haven't eaten in a week.

Earlier, I'd had eggs, bacon, couple of English muffins with butter and real peach marmalade. Hell, I'm almost human again. The best Vegas casinos have always been able to sling some seriously good food around, and the Magnum is definitely one of the best. I've always believed that breakfast, and I ain't talking about bean sprout yogurt and fresh broccoli juice here, is a highly underrated meal.

I had needed that, too. Not just because of me being "overserved" last night, as my daddy used to say. The Maker's Mark just kept coming, so what was I supposed to do? Oh hell no, it was also because of what had happened earlier in the evening at the final table.

There had been only five card players left at the beginning of the round. When it was over, there would be only two who would play tonight for the WPA Gold Bracelet and about ten million in cash.

The room phone rings, and I almost spill my coffee. Who in the hell do I want to talk to right now? That's an easy answer, and I just let it go. Looking at my watch again, I finish the last swallow and then pour another cup.

I'm pacing all around the suite and finally walk back to the wall of glass. The morning paper is on the bed. I'd tried that already. Nothing will do but to drag my ass back through the flames again, so I just need to finish this painful little recap, I guess.

Kenny Whitten had been so pissed off when he had gone out that he went straight through the ballroom doors to the airport. Didn't say y'all can kiss my ass, go to hell or nothin'. His girlfriend had been left to pack everything up and had to meet him at the airport. He's always been that way, a little California brat, just a pouting little baby. Tried to run everyone off with straight bluff. To his credit, it did look like he had it, and he sure bet it up, but you know this is poker and he wasn't the only poker player sitting around that table. I ran away from the hand, had absolutely nothing to stay with anyway and everyone else folded too, but old Larry stayed and broke Kenny like a dry twig.

Next to be booted out, not even ten minutes later, was Karl Steiner from Germany. Nice enough guy, but hell, luckier than shit just to get to the televised rounds. Went all in on two pair, and he was looking strong right up to the end until I hit that third eight I needed on the flop.

That left three players. Yours truly here, Larry Mantrell from Ada, Oklahoma, and René Gaust from Lyon, France.

Larry was old-school, a gentleman and had been playing for forty years. He used to give Doyle Brunson a go for his money way back in the day. He's still damn good, but he's old and shaky. This week has been like his one last hurrah. It's been a magical kind of tournament for him. Cards when he needs them, plenty of luck, and everything he tries, he hits. He hasn't made the final table for years.

Then there's René Gaust. Sweet René, as I call him, just to piss him off, is someone who's just so damn easy to hate. He has the normal snooty-ass French arrogance thing going, basically dismissing everyone around him as some breed of dog. Truly a French blueblood, his family is loaded and connected throughout Europe. Along with over two centuries of continued, inherited wealth, they own the majority stock of the single largest telecommunications company in France.

And oh yeah, he's young, really young. Twenty, I think. Women love him, always a couple hanging on him. Baseball cap on backward, dresses like a high school kid, which he almost is, wears earphones and sunglasses to hide his eyes. He's a talker during games too, heavy accent, almost constant chattering. Trying to distract, to anger or to get your nerves all jangled up.

Did I mention the little bastard is good? Probably the best all-around card player I've ever seen, if he keeps playing like he does now. I mean, I'm only thirty-one, a professional for a short five years, so it's not like I have all these big rivalries yet. But Gaust is one of maybe four or five top players that I just can't quite completely figure out.

I've won a lot of money already, and I won the big dance, the World Championship, right here last year. I plan on winning a lot more, so if there's anyone I want to beat and beat bad, like scrub the floor with him bad, its guys like Sweet René. Spoiled little rich, French prick. Other than that, he's an okay guy.

QUEEN OF DIAMONDS

A chirp breaks up my miserable memories of last night. My cell rings this time, and I look to see who it is. It's not Laura like I thought, though, and I don't recognize the area code. I let it go to voicemail.

Laura and I probably ain't gonna work out. In fact, forget the probably, as much as I wish it wasn't true. She's gotten pretty damn tired of me flying all over creation, and I've gotten pretty damn tired of her, period. This is not her world, and it never will be. San Antonio is her whole world. I'm kind of with her on that, but I hate to break it to my little Laura that there are about ten more years of this deal yet to play out. Growing up the way I did and seeing my dad bust his ass to get paid nothing, I'm never going back to living like that.

I gotta say this, I'm having a helluva lot of fun. Playing cards all around the U.S. and the world for that matter. Beating silver-spoon assholes while I'm at it. Making damn good money, eating better than the King of Siam, drinking the best there is, playing hard and I'm not talking cards all the time, staying at the finest hotels and sleeping until noon when I can sleep. What doesn't work for you in that list?

Laura just wants to have a family and go to high school football games again. That blonde girl that's in the other room right now, though? The one all tangled up in those satin sheets? Well, she just wants to have fun. That's kind of where I'm at right now. My mind hangs on Laura for a second because we've always been together. Always, being since we were seniors in High School.

She just doesn't hold me anymore though, and my mind drifts back to sitting at that table last night. Three of us. We had been playing for over an hour since Steiner had been bounced from the table. Old Larry is short stacked, with René holding the chip lead over me, but not by much as we both keep winning hands.

Larry's not getting cards, and he's folding a lot. On the other hand, I had just won a quarter-million-dollar hand with a jack high. Hey, this is poker and that's the way it is. Larry is getting desperate now and that's never a good thing.

Frank Zafiro and Jim Wilsky

The old man suddenly and firmly goes all in on a hand. He's always been a hard read, because he's got that tired old hangdog look and he doesn't help you with other tells, either. Winning or losing, he just looks like he's beat to shit and ready to die. I look at René right away because at this point I don't really care what Larry has in his hand. What matters here is what the little French asshole on my right is going to do.

"Ahhh now, what do you have there, my old, *old* friend? Hmmm?" René gives Larry a sneer and laughs quietly. "Nothing. That's clear." The Frenchman looks at his two cards, the table, at Larry and back again. Then he waves a hand at me and shrugs without even looking at me. "And my big Texan here, *pfft*, what does it matter what you have, eh?"

We sit through about five minutes of that bullshit and then Sweet René just folds.

René wanted me to play him, and maybe even lose, because he knew that I wouldn't just give it to Larry. It would be too bloody for him to get in with both of us. Why risk it? He had the chip lead and knew he'd most likely be playing me for the championship tomorrow night anyway.

The Frenchman was right. It would be him and me. I had two pair, sevens and aces. Larry could have something I guess, but I just didn't see it. He was done, and it was just a matter of time.

"I'm in." I say it casually and slide over what I need to match Larry in the pot. I still have some chips left of course, but until I slide all of it back this way I have two stacks instead of six.

When I saw Larry's eyes sag a little more, oh so slightly, I knew he had been bluffing.

He flipped his cards on the table, and I couldn't believe it. Nothing at all. A king and a six of diamonds. If you're short stacked you've gotta jump out there but *damn*. He was just gassed, I guess. I mean, he did look tired, almost sick. Must've just wanted out. Hey, third place pays damn good at the championship final table.

"Oh myyyy, Larreeee. King high, that's eet? Hey, Tex,

whatchoo got, eh?" René could never just shut the hell up even if he folded a hand.

I flipped my two cards, and Larry nodded his head slowly and smiled at me. He looked so damn beaten right then. It had to be sad to the people watching at home. Great drama. The old pro, the new breed, bad guys, good guys. Truth be known, I don't really feel bad for people in situations like this. Not even Larry. I really, honestly, don't care. This is a fucking card game, not a support group.

"Good luck, Larry." I nod back to him with great understanding and humility, sounding just sincere as hell. After all, it's who Cord Needham is to people. I'm the good guy. I wear a fine Resistol cowboy hat everywhere I go, but I take it off at the table as gentlemen do.

René chuckles to himself.

The dealer deals. Burns and turns.

The turn card is a damn king. The crowd cheers, whoops and hollers for a while and then quiets. René whistles softly.

I'm wearing just a small, good-hearted smile but thinking to myself, *Jesus, of all the damn cards in the deck*. I keep smiling too because I know the camera will be on me at some point.

I look at Larry, and he calmly sits and waits. He doesn't stand up and run his hands through his hair or pace around all crazy as some of these new kids like to do when they go all in. He just sits there with his palms flat on the green felt and smiles that sad smile. Awaits his fate.

He's dead and he knows it.

I'm thinking no way. No way another king.

The dealer pauses for a little longer than normal, then burns and turns the river card. The king of spades.

The audience erupts, and the dealer slides the huge pot over to Larry.

Such is poker, ladies and gents. I had no business losing that hand and poor sad old Larry, who looked like he had one foot in the grave earlier, had no business winning the next five hands either. Big pots too. I couldn't pull any cards after that cowboy hand of Larry's. The well just went dry. Even René got a little quiet.

On the sixth hand, I went all in on nothing. I had to. Ace high. I was beaten by an inside straight that Larry pulled out of his ass on the river card. Again. Somehow, I was out of the tournament. Gone. Larry and René would play for the championship tomorrow night.

I never leave the table too quickly. I shake all the hands, pat the shoulders, and give a wave to the crowd. I did not vary my routine last night, but I sure wanted to.

With a little jerk, I snap out of my little flashback and realize I'm looking out the window again. Well, tonight is that championship.

"Cord?" a soft voice from behind me. Even softer hands around my waist.

"Yeah?" I purposely try to sound pissed and bored, although I'm really neither.

"Would you like some company today? We could just hang out together for a bit, maybe? No commits or nothing at all, really. Just hang out?"

"That probably ain't gonna work out too good, darlin'. I've got a couple of meetings and tournament appearances today, so I'll have to get going on things pretty quick. Sorry, but you know how it is."

"Yeah, I know. I get it. I'll leave you my number, just in case you have some time tonight. You want to have some breakfast before I go?"

"Already ate."

"Sure. Sure, okay, well, just give me a few minutes."

"No problem, but I do have to get going here pretty quick." I have nothing to do, but she needs to leave. I don't even know her name.

"Sure, okay, Cord."

QUEEN OF DIAMONDS

At some point today, I really will have to do some things. Get back down there and show myself. Circulate a little bit. Hang out at the regular casino tables a little bit. The association expects that out of the big boys, and they make it worth your while. Besides, it's good marketing. Big smiles, shake hands, and slowly shake my head sadly. Then give them that smile again and shrug my shoulders. Maybe that trademark, soft, "aw shucks" laugh.

First, I'm going to get in a steaming hot shower for a good twenty minutes with the dial switched to the hardest needle spray I can find.

THREE
Casey

"I'm just saying, Casey. That's all."

Babe Parcella stared at me from across his huge metal desk, his expression open and friendly. I knew this guy had more faces than a store full of clocks, so I didn't entirely buy that he was being sincere. But at the same time, he was doing me a solid here, so that put me in a tough spot.

"It's not like I'm her boss," I told him cautiously.

A tolerant smile creased the big man's lips. "Not saying that. But you're practically married to her, right? You could say something."

I raised my eyebrows at that. Married? Not even close. I don't think that word even exists in Nicky's vocabulary. Mostly, I think I was her guilty pleasure, or a way to have someone without being beholden to anyone. Or maybe I was just a warm body and a stiff cock. Hell if I knew.

What I did know was that I couldn't just go and ask her to back off on Babe Parcella and the Magnum casino. That would go over like a bad beat at the final table.

But I couldn't tell this huge son of a bitch no, either.

Babe was still watching me. His eerie similarity to Babe Ruth always put me a little on edge. On the one hand, it was familiar, because I grew up seeing those pictures and videos of home runs, him waving to the crowd and so forth. But Babe Parcella had the eyes of a predator, whereas George Herman Ruth had the eyes of a partier. Or maybe a sad clown. Still, it was weird, having one of your childhood heroes stare at you like he might decide to crack your skull just as soon as he'd shake your hand.

Yeah, I know he isn't *the* Babe, but he's the only Babe in my world these days, and goddamn if he isn't one scary dude.

"Case? You go to sleep on me here?"

I took a deep breath and shook my head. "Nah. I'm just thinking it through. I mean, for Nicky, the job is her life. She's addicted."

"So get her more addicted to your Johnson instead," Babe suggested mildly, but his eyes narrowed slightly. He reached out and adjusted the nameplate on his desk. I knew it was to call my attention to the title under his name. Head of Casino Security. Mr. Big Shot, at least at the Magnum. "That oughta be easy enough. You're in her bed already."

But not in her head, I figured. Probably not her heart, either.

"Unless you don't want to help," Babe said. "Unless that's it."

"No, that's not it," I assured him.

"Because I helped you out here with your little problem, right?" He smiled tightly. "So I'm not seeing where me asking you this small favor is such a monumental fucking deal."

"I appreciate what you're doing," I said, looking down at the stack of chips on the desk between us. "You know I'm just in a cold stretch, is all. It's going to snap soon. They always do."

Babe kept smiling but the grin didn't touch his eyes. "Not always. Not for everyone."

A cold tickle brushed the base of my spine and climbed my back. I cleared my throat. "It always has for me, Babe. You know that. You've seen it."

He nodded slowly. "Yeah, I've seen it. Even back in the day. After that thing."

I knew exactly what he meant. Back when I was catching in the minor leagues. Signed by the Phillies and working my way up toward the big club. Until I blew out my knee in practice. At least, that was the story we gave to the Phils. I wondered if Babe knew the truth. He probably did.

"Yeah," I said. "I guess it wasn't meant to be."

"But you bounced back. You always bounce back." He gestured toward the chips. "That's why I know you're good for that."

I tried not to sigh. He had me. As long as I was at a table and in a money game, the vultures would stay back. If I stopped showing up at the tables, they'd swoop in and I'd lose a lot more than a career in the majors. I needed this line of credit, and he fucking knew it.

"I'm good for it," I said.

"Like I said, I know."

We were quiet for a moment. Then I said, "Look, I'll work on her, okay? But she doesn't listen to me so much on work-related stuff." Truth was, she barely talked about it at all and never asked my advice on so much as where to park.

Babe shrugged. "Just say something to her. That's all I'm asking. She's not your puppet, right? You can't make her do what you want. You can only talk to her. You can only suggest. You can only point her in the right direction. It's up to her to make the smart choice."

He didn't mean that at all, and we both knew it. "I can try," I said. "She can be a handful, though. Headstrong."

"What woman isn't?"

I could have named a couple hundred in this town without pausing to think, but arguing with Babe Parcella is a losing bet.

"Probably none," I agreed instead.

"So, you'll take care of this for me?"

"I'll try," I said.

He stared at me for another long moment, then nodded his head. "All right. Good to hear." He stood and held out a hand the size of an Easter ham. "Always nice to see you, Case."

I rose and took his hand. He squeezed it just hard enough to make his point, but not too hard to be obvious about it.

"Good luck at the tables," he added.

I nodded my thanks, scooped the chips off his desk, and walked out of his office before he changed his mind.

FOUR
Cord

We've been out here in the huge mezzanine area for at least an hour just bullshitting around with onlookers, fans, and the media.

I peek back through the sets of large open doors that lead into the grand ballroom where the finals are being held again tonight. It's pretty much a ghost town in there now. Just a couple of goofs walking around pointing at shit up in the ceiling. A few light guys, sound guys and the like, scurrying around.

Mack Reynolds and I had been in there earlier. He was the face and television announcer for all of the World Poker Association events. We had already wrapped up the scheduled interview. With all the fluffy director comments from behind the camera, lighting problems and assorted bullshit, plus Mack screwing up the questions, it took about an hour and a half.

The final table, dramatically lit up, had been used as a backdrop, and Mack had asked me how this thing would unfold tonight, the strategies, the playing styles, who would be favored, blah, blah blah.

"What are we doing now, boss?" I ask while shaking another strangers' hand and then signing an ace of spades for some guy.

"Not much more, Cord. Well, not here, anyway," Ronnie says without looking at me.

Ronnie Turnbull is my marketing guy, travel coordinator, agent, legal advisor, consultant and accountant. And best friend.

He's been with me since I won my first average-size tournament in Shreveport almost four years ago.

That same year, not even two months later, I got my second big win and a much bigger payday. This was at the Aruba Royale Casino and Resort. It could have been my *last* win, my last *night* in fact, if Ronnie wouldn't have been there.

We had us a little impromptu, wild-ass private beach party to celebrate the win. It was very late. There were two young ladies, and everything was good at first, but then an ex-boyfriend who also happened to be an ex-con showed up. With him was a brother of the other girl. Both guys were drunk. Both were pissed. There was a very long knife and a shorter one involved. Ronnie had saved my ass.

He got us out of there that night and got us an iron-clad alibi too. There was an investigation later, but it was never even tied to us. It was all hung on the ex-con old boyfriend. Gotta admit, the guy was railroaded all the way. Needless to say, we've never been back to that Aruba tournament.

Ronnie and I had grown up together in San Antonio. We were friends before I even knew what a flush straight was. There is no one else in this world I trust more than him. Including myself.

"Ohhhh myyy," he chuckles to me now as some painted up, big-haired gal is making a beeline for us through the crowd. "Y'all be nice now...then, we're out of here."

"Cord! Cord Needham!"

The woman is probably fifty or so and trying hard, too hard, to look thirty. In my mind, there ain't nothing worse than that.

"Well, hello there, darlin'," I say to her, smiling that smile. Ronnie turns and walks away quickly. He laughs but covers it with a cough.

"Oh. My. *GOD*! I'm Patty Donovan. Howard and I watched you on television last year when you won this damn thing. I said right then and there, I said, we are coming here this year and watching that Cord Needham in person!"

She hands an expensive-looking camera to her husband, no

doubt Howard, and then prances over to me. Putting a hand around my waist, she shoved her considerable and fake boobs into my ribs and hugged me tight. "Just one quick shot, Cord! Just one picture!"

After the fourth picture, I am signing the back of her damn shirt, but then Ronnie rescues me by pretending we are running late and he skillfully excuses us.

Now listen, don't get me wrong here. I ain't Peyton Manning or Kobe Bryant. This is the poker world, not the NFL or NBA. It's not like I have to fight my way through the wild throngs of fans everywhere I go.

But, I will say this. This is Vegas, this is big-time, high-stakes poker, and I do have some fans. You'd be amazed probably. I have endorsements and sell things with my name on it. So, basically, Peyton and Kobe can kiss my ass, 'cause I'm doing just fine.

On the elevator down, Ronnie gets on the phone again. He's talking to someone in Atlantic City about the Champions Tournament coming up. Arguing about something, then agreeing and then arguing again.

"All right, pardner," he says after signing off the call, "Let's go sit with the little people. You can schmooze and play some bullshit cards and thrill everybody with your mastery of the game. Then we're done. Promise. Another hour or two in the casino and we're done."

I look at the ceiling and don't say anything right away. This sucks, like I knew it would and like it always does. It's all part of the ride we're riding and just a part of the game, but damn it, sometimes this shit gets really old. Hey, if I was playing for another bracelet and all the marbles tonight? Well hell, that's different, it would make all of this bullshit much easier to swallow. The fact is, though, I ain't playing tonight and this isn't easy.

"We got a deal?" he says. "Two more hours in the casino, have a couple casual drinks, and before you know it we're all done. Hell, maybe you and I go and get a couple big-ass steaks somewhere tonight. Steaks as big as manhole covers. Just us, like the old days?"

I look at him and narrow my eyes. He always knows what I'm thinking. Well, except for Laura. He's clueless on that. Oh sure, he knows about all the women and girls on the side, it's just that he still figures at some point it'll be me and Laura settling down and getting married.

But he knows where I'm at right now.

"Then we have a few drinks and come back here to watch that little fucking French frog beat the shit out of poor old Larry. Whattya say, pard?"

"Sure. Sure, Ronnie. Just start that two-hour stopwatch right now, though, okay?"

"You got it."

With perfect timing, the elevator doors slide open and we walk toward the casino entrance.

I swear there will never be a time I get tired of casinos. Sure, I get tired of what we're doing right now, but just the pure gambling in casinos? To me, it's the ultimate high.

We walk in and I immediately see familiar faces everywhere: some standing around, some playing, and some others just milling.

Ronnie and I get a drink from the waitress and cruise around a little. We move slowly, but we're always moving. It's better that way.

Sooner or later, I'll sit down somewhere at one of the higher limit tables, but not with the big dogs. All the casinos and the Association love it when you mingle with what I call the upper middle class of poker players.

Casinos want the whales for sure, but where they really make their money is with semi-pros, tourists, and people who know how to play cards. They also have some money and are looking to throw it around. Even if they do win, though, they won't break the bank.

I don't care where it is or with who it is, anytime I sit down to play Hold 'Em, it's serious business. There ain't no messing around. I'm out to take everybody's money. Then again, this kind of deal today is more like an exhibition match. Sure, I play to win, but I take it easy on folks and they know better than to try and run me, too. That's just the way it is.

"Whoa, now."

"What?" Ronnie turns to me and frowns. "What's wrong?" As he says it, his eyes follow mine to two tables over, on our left.

A big whoop lets out, and a girl claps her hands over her head. I can tell from here that she's hotter than a two-dollar pistol.

The dealer shoves a pot pile her way, and she laughs out loud again. Starts stacking her chips and smiles all sexy at one of the other players.

"See?" Ronnie says. "There you go. This won't be such a bad two hours, right?"

So, having picked my table, I amble my way over and Ronnie graciously asks if it would be alright if I join the table for a bit. Just for a while now, because good old Cord here has got another engagement at four thirty and he can't be late...

I pull out a chair. "I sure appreciate everyone here letting me barge in and play for a bit."

"Like we got a choice," a big guy grumbles on my left but then sticks his hand out quickly and finishes, "but I can't think of another pro I'd rather lose to more! Big fan of yours, Cord. I'm Mike Conrad, from Scottsdale."

"A pleasure, Mike."

Out of the corner of my eye, I see Ronnie drift off to get another drink. He's evidently surveyed the table and is satisfied with the smiles all around.

Around the table of six players it goes, with everyone saying hello and all of them recognizing who the hell I am. Except of course for the reason I picked this table to begin with. I can tell she doesn't know who I am, and on top of that, could give a shit.

She's on my far right with an empty chair between us, and she is looking at me with about the most beautiful green eyes I've ever seen. The look is flat though, almost no emotion. Like a shark, with green eyes, if that makes any sense.

"Cord?"

"Yes, ma'am."

"No, I mean is that right? Cord or Cort?"

"Oh, it's Cord, with a 'd.' Cord Needham, San Antonio, Texas, and it's awful nice to make your acquaintance."

She says nothing more, just toys with a couple of chips. Stacks them, unstacks them, rolls them over and between her fingers. Little nervous ticks that card players do.

"Sorry, I just don't keep up with pro poker players. Don't know you, but I can tell by everyone else here that you're a *very* pretty important guy."

"Not hardly." I just keep smiling despite the smart-ass comment and reached my hand out. "I didn't catch your name, and if I don't get it from you, I'm not gonna sleep well at all tonight."

She finally smiles at that and almost laughs, but it's a knowing smile. It's a look that says "Okay, I liked that one, but don't try any more of that homespun bullshit with me, buck." There is also something more, a little danger just under the surface with this girl.

"Annie."

"Hello there, Annie. You play a lot?"

"A lot. Poker you mean, right?" She blinked big and innocent, her eyebrows go up playfully.

"Uhh, yes. Poker."

"Well, not here. Never here in Vegas, but yes, I like to play. My dad taught me when I was young. He was very…tricky." She smiles longer and better this time.

"Okay, great. Well hell, everybody, let's play us a few hands before I got to run." I look around the table at everyone and take my hat off, straighten my gold championship bracelet on my wrist and motion for a waitress.

* * *

Dealer deals. I don't look at my hole cards yet, though. I hold my hand up dramatically.

"One last thing, folks. Take it easy on me here. I can't go walking out of here with my pockets hanging out, okay? Bad for the reputation, so ease the hell up." I say it every time, and it works every time.

Good old Mike Conrad from Scottsdale Arizona chuckles, and I can tell he's thinking this is just about the best damn day of his life.

Annie hasn't taken her eyes off of me either. But those eyes that are checking me out are poker eyes. Oh, she's loosened up and smiling more now but…*Why, you little bitch. You're gonna try me, aren't you?*

Not quite an hour later, she has doubled up on everybody except me, and one poor bastard has already looked at his watch and said, "man I gotta go." Although time had nothing at all to do with his leaving.

She is betting heavy and hard, pressing the limit with every bump. Raising over me whenever she can.

Just now I had trip nines, and she hit trip jacks on the river. Another hand lost, and another sizeable pot goes to her. She does her little whoop again.

"Well *damn*, Annie." I sit back and sigh with disgust. "You ought to be over at the high limit tables 'stead a wastin' your time on us."

The guy sitting next to Annie on the other side speaks up. He's getting steamed and staring holes through her. "Yeah, hot streaks are great while they last, I 'spose. Sooner or later, though…"

When the new hand is dealt, she barely even looks at her two hole cards and bets it big.

"This is how I play. This is no streak."

I have a suited big slick in the hole this time. That don't always mean something. In fact, it can be a heartbreaker as many times as not. I stay for now, but I'm ready to blow on the flop. I'm watching her, though, getting a little more used to her.

She boats, and I lose again, along with some old boy who just joined the game and stayed like a dumbass. Dealer deals. I motion the waitress.

Ronnie walks over to the table and hovers. He catches my eye without saying a word.

He points to his watch and shrugs his shoulders as in "What's it going to be, pard? Go or stay?" He takes a casual sip of his drink and glances at Annie.

I look at my two cards.

Three of spades and a snowman. Fuck me.

I look up at Ronnie and shake my head no as I look back at my cards. I got no business staying on this hand. "I'll see the five hundred."

I give Ronnie a grin and proceed to lose another hand. There is another short, quick whoop from Annie. I just missed hitting an inside straight on that last hand, but I could tell she didn't see or really care to know what I had been up to.

Her stacks of chips look like the fucking skyline of Manhattan. She can't stop straightening them and shifting or sliding them carefully around. It's a nervous, fidgety, and compulsive type of movement. It's a holy shit look at all this fuckin' money, type of movement. Fun to watch.

I shake my head sadly at Annie and give her my best hangdog look. In return, she finally gives me the look I've been waiting for. The one she doesn't even know she's giving. It's a certain little glint in the eye and a very hot vibe. I ain't talking about some potential dancing in the sheets later vibe, although I sure don't want to throw that out the window or anything.

No, I'm talking about that look a player gets at the very peak of his or her run. The fever when it reaches one hundred and five. Sometimes it takes two days, sometimes it takes two hours, like Annie here. The Apex. The brightest this light is gonna get before it goes out. In other words, there's no other direction to go now except back down the other side of the mountain. I would have been happy to just watch her ride this little streak and then leave. This attitude she has though, I just gotta stay a little while longer.

Oh man, do I love this game. As the new cards are sliding out to us she shoots a quick look over at me. Almost like she just heard what I was thinking.

So I meet her eyes and whispered silently.

Okay little sister, let's really play some cards now.

FIVE
Casey

I stared across the table at Pipe Guy.

Yeah, I know that isn't exactly original, but playing the tourist tables isn't something I do to build relationships. Or to waste time learning names. The guy across the table from me was the only one left in the hand. He chewed on a droopy, deep dark brown pipe. My guess is that he figured it made him look like he had style. Or hell, maybe he thought it was a distraction.

What it was, was ridiculous. But ridiculous money spends the same as cool money, so I stayed in the hand. I needed to take this little tremble of good luck that had begun earlier in the night and see if it swelled into a wave. Then I'd go to the bigger tables.

The thing about luck, at least for me, is that it is never about the size of the wager. It's either riding hot or it's not. I could be playing penny slots or sitting at the big table with old Larry Mantrell and that pompous ass René Gaust, and my luck would play out the same. Like I said, it's a wave, and if it was hot luck, then I had to ride it hard and high until it crashed against the shore.

Bad luck? Gotta ride out that shit, too. It's just the nature of the world.

So here I was, nursing a whiskey coke, trying to beat out some guy who was probably a TV salesman back in his home-town. Or maybe a plumber. You couldn't barely call it money, what we were playing for. But after losing most of what Babe gave me, I'd started taking it steady from Pipe Guy for the last hour. Cud Chewer and Unibrow had lost their fair share, too. I could feel the luck wave rumbling upward. One more good win and I'd be up on that board, hanging ten all the way over to the tables where they played for Ben Franklin instead of Honest Abe.

I probably would've left two hands ago, but it was just about to be my turn through the blinds and leaving at that point is pretty poor form. Unless you bust out, of course.

It wasn't that I cared if any of these working-class mopes thought I was an asshole. Karma cared, though, and she could fuck with my luck wave, so I kicked in my chips for the blinds and played through both hands. Then I announced that the next one would be my last.

"What?" Unibrow said. "You gotta stay and give me a chance to win my money back."

I felt like telling him that neither of us had enough time left on this planet for him to do that, but I settled for a tight smile.

"It's a girl," Cud Chewer said, grinning wide. His huge wad of gum danced around his mouth while he stared at me. "Ain't it?"

I didn't answer.

"Tell the truth," he continued. "You got some tail waiting for ya, huh?"

I glanced over at the dealer and waited.

"Asshole," whispered Cud Chewer, and not too quietly.

The dealer, a thirty-two-year-old Filipina named Tala, glanced at him and then back at me. Her face was impassive, but I knew she was sizing up the problem. One more red flag, and she'd wave the pit boss over.

I held up one finger. "One last hand. Just so no one thinks I'm rude."

"Too late," Cud Chewer said.

Like some kind of superhero, Gregory appeared at the table. As security goes, the only guy scarier than Gregory is the Babe himself. If the man was under six-two, then René Gaust wasn't

French. On top of that, two and a half bills was a conservative estimate for him, and almost none of it was fat.

"Problem?" he asked softly. Gregory always spoke in quiet tones. Hell, half the time, I don't think people heard a word he said. They already knew they were being wrong in some way, and they took one look at him and summarily unfucked themselves. He probably could have recited poetry to troublemakers, and they'd never realize it. They just saw the size, and they straightened right up.

Cud Chewer was smarter than he looked. "Nope," he said. He drained his Budweiser, stood, gathered his chips, and walked away without looking back.

Gregory gave a nod and moved on. Probably off to catch a comet or something.

So Tala dealt. I didn't bother looking at my cards right away. Instead, I watched everyone get theirs. No one had shit, except maybe Pipe Guy, who immediately tossed in. Unibrow stayed too, but then again, he had the big blind. Everyone else slid their useless cards back to Tala.

I picked up mine.

Ace. King. And suited, too.

Feel the wave, I thought.

A lot of guys don't like to see these cards. Some even call it the Anna Kournikova. As in, looks great but rarely wins. Me? I figured it's a good start.

I tossed in my chips, making it a threesome.

Tala burned and turned. The flop was terrible. Off-suited crap that didn't help me a bit. Unibrow, either, I figured, since he folded immediately.

Pipe Guy fiddled with his silly pipe, eyeballing me. I stared back at him, letting him think he was getting something. One thing I'm good at is my poker face. I give them nothing. It's saved my ass on more than a few occasions when luck had abandoned me. Pipe Guy wasn't going to get a whiff.

He finally smiled knowingly, like he'd just discovered the secret to Sir Francis Drake's treasure, and pushed in two full stacks of chips. It wasn't big money in the real world, but it was big enough for this table, and it was half of what he had left.

I looked back down at the flop. No pairs, nothing touching for a straight. I suppose he could be vying for that, but he'd need a least one more card to make it happen. Flush-wise, there were two clubs out, so he could be sitting on two of his own and hoping to hit another. But that was an awful big bet for someone who couldn't have shit in his hand just yet.

Unless, of course, he had a pocket pair that matched up. Hell, that would give him trips already.

And me and my sexy tennis player weren't looking so hot.

But this was my last hand. And I wasn't going to fold.

"Call." I slid my chips in and asked the poker gods to be kind to my swelling baby wave.

Tala burned. She turned.

Another bullet. And a heart, too. Couldn't see how that helped Pipe Guy, but he grinned all mysteriously and pushed the rest of his stack into the middle.

"All in."

I could still feel the warm flush of luck. It wasn't going to subside because some pretentious TV salesman with a pipe from Akron or Newark or fucking Sacramento had trips shit in his hand. Or if he was bluffing. No way.

"Call."

Pipe Guy smiled and turned his cards over. Pocket sevens, marrying up to the one from the flop.

"Trip sevens," he announced, like I was blind or something.

"Three of a kind," Tala announced, making it official. "Sevens."

I rolled over mine.

"Pair," Tala said. "Aces."

There was a flicker of concern that crossed his face just then, but to his credit, he covered it up pretty fast. He knew there were only two cards out there that could beat him. And who knows, maybe someone dumped those off the deal or the burns.

But I wasn't worried. I felt good. I was going to win and then go hit the large tables, and before I knew it, I'd be up serious money. Then I could pay off the Swede, or at least put him at bay, and get back in the black.

Tala expertly flipped away the burn card. I watched the river come, but I already knew what I'd see.

Ace of clubs.

A small roar went up from the half dozen people watching. I grinned and raked in my chips.

Pipe Guy shook his head ruefully.

I stacked up a hundred in chips and handed it to Tala.

"Thank you, sir," she said as if she didn't know me. As if she hadn't been dealing to me for years. As if that weekend in Phoenix had been someone else.

But that's the game. It's all Vegas.

I took my modest haul and headed toward the big tables. What I'd won would barely stake me to a real game, but it didn't matter.

My luck had turned.

I stopped by the cage and cashed out. Call it superstitious, but I always liked to buy fresh chips at a new table. What can I say? Every gambler has his thing.

When I turned away from the cashier, I bumped into Mats. The small, wiry man is easy to miss at first, but once you get a look at him, he's suddenly impossible not to see. His hand lashed out and clamped onto my wrist before I could put the cash into my front pocket. His strong, bony fingers dug into my flesh.

"What you got there, Casey boy?" he whispered in a voice as greasy as his slicked-back hair. "Something for the Swede, maybe?"

The Swede was Viktor Stahlberg, but I don't think anyone

outside of the cops and a few of us who have been in the game for a long while knew his real name. To most everyone, he was just "the Swede." And most everyone owed him money at one time or another.

"It's just a little stake money," I told Mats, staring back at his flat, beady gaze. "I'm on a roll. I'm headed to the big tables to run it up. I'll have something for the Swede by morning."

Mats shook his head, clucking his tongue. "Foolish Casey. You always try to get yourself out of the hole by digging some more. When has that ever worked?"

"I'll have the money."

He squeezed my wrist even harder, twisting it and pulling my hand toward him. My grip on the small wad of cash loosened, and he plucked the money from my palm. Behind us, the cashier was doing his best impression of a blind statue.

Mats flipped through the bills, his eyes doing a quick count. Then he shook his head in disgust. "Not even close, Casey. Not even close."

"It's stake money," I repeated. "I took it off the tourist tables."

"This kind of money?" Mats held up the cash. "For this, you should just get a regular job. Sell cars or computers. Or for you, maybe coach little league, heh?"

I clenched my jaw. "I'm a poker player."

"You're a credit risk is what you are, *pojke*."

"I'm always good for it."

"So far."

I held out my hand. "There isn't even enough there to pay for one of the Swede's trips to the Derringer Club upstairs. But it'll stake me. And I'll use it to get his money."

Mats watched me while he considered. Finally, he shrugged and held the cash out to me. When I reached for it, he pulled it back, smiling to expose his rat teeth. Christ, in the casino lighting, they were even yellow.

He peeled off five hundred and slid it into his jacket pocket. "That's the vig on the vig," he said, handing me the rest.

I stuffed the money in my pocket. "You mean it's your cut to leave me the fuck alone. Does the Swede know about that little angle of yours?"

He glared at me. "Always the smart mouth with you, Casey."

I knew I'd pay for what I'd just said the next time we were someplace darker or less populated. Right then, I didn't care. Most days, Mats the Rat would have walked off with my entire stake, and the next time we met, he'd act like it had never happened. Meanwhile, the points on my debt would continue to accumulate.

Not tonight, though. Because tonight, my luck was up. So I could afford a smart remark.

Probably.

"I gotta go," I said, and brushed past him.

True to my luck, he let me go.

I wandered toward the larger tables, but at an easy pace. Sometimes it pays to stroll past the different tables to see what's happening. There might be a particular vibe that I catch or an easy mark that jumps out at me. It can be worth the time. Besides, this was Vegas. Time didn't mean shit.

When I saw her, it was at the expensive tables, but not the ones the whales played at. This table was for the higher end amateurs, the ones who knew what they were doing as well as someone outside of the game can know it. She was smiling, and even in a city full of gorgeous women, there was something beautiful and smoldering in her green eyes that stopped me cold. I didn't know what grabbed me, but at the same time, I felt it as strong and as real as the cash in my pocket.

She was raking a decent-sized pot toward her. A small crowd had gathered, and there was polite clapping and a little bit of light laughter.

I moved closer and stood near an empty seat. She cocked her

head my direction, almost as if she'd sensed my arrival. A moment later, our eyes met. She gave me a secretive smile and looked away.

For a moment, I thought about talking to her. Then I blushed, embarrassed at the thought. What was I, some grade schooler with a love note? Do you like me, check yes or no?

Then I wanted to sit down and get dealt in, because then it would be okay to talk to her if I wanted. That was poker. I could find out her name, maybe her story. Maybe I could read that face some more and figure out why she was such a crushing beauty. Why I felt drawn to her like every cliché in every bad romance movie.

Come on, I wanted to shout at myself. *Are you kidding me?* I'd been a jock in high school and then in the pros. Sure, it wasn't the majors, but the women were there, and in ample numbers. Never had a problem with that. Even after that all ended, I had something that worked. A hint of a bad boy in clean clothes or something. Hell, it even worked on Nicky, and she was a detective, and tough.

Nicky. Shit.

I put her out of my mind. I wanted to meet this girl in front of me, the one who was checking her cards now with easy confidence before she glanced over at me again.

Oh yeah, I wanted to talk to her. Or sit and play. Or fucking grovel at her feet.

What I did was stand there and watch her play and say nothing.

SIX
Cord

Right now, it's just the three of us. Everyone else has scattered because the money had gotten pretty serious, and most people don't exactly want to sit with Cord Needham when tall stacks of purples chips are sliding around.

On a pair of cowboys, she takes her first hand since about an hour ago. The cute little whoop she just let out didn't have the same life to it anymore.

Her stacks had shrunk and mine had grown about the same amount. I always run a total in my head, and she'd lost almost exactly two-thirds of what she had when I first sat down. Lover Boy was even worse off. He was about done—or about ready to buy-in on more chips.

"Man, them cowboys are everywhere today, mainly in your hands." Casey Somebody smiled and laughed. I think my name for him, Lover Boy, fits him better. He's just all in love and shit with Annie. Sturdy, good-looking guy probably played ball of some sort but cards don't give a damn about any of that.

He had finally sat down about a half hour ago after standing there and just watching her. I figure he might be a fairly regular player here. He had that Vegas look about him. Some people seemed to know him, and I'm pretty sure he knew who I was.

"Do you come here often, Annie? Because if you do, warn me next time." He was all but drooling.

"Hey, the pro over there is the one you need to watch. He's finally getting hot." She laughed, but it was an empty cough.

It was clear to me that cards had taken a backseat for ol' Lover Boy, at least for a bit. Every move Annie made was the most amazing thing he'd ever seen. Not just card moves. Hell, anything.

Funny as shit to watch, and I can't blame him, but it's a golden rule, you can't chase tail and play real money poker. Hey, I'm a huntin' dog, too, but you can't do both at the same time if you're a serious card player.

"Those cowboys are hot, though, and I do love hot cowboys." She winks at him and shows him the dimples. "Hey, listen, I need about five minutes, boys." She looks at us and then gets up, slinging a bag over her shoulder. "I'll be right back. Save my seat, 'kay?"

"Uh, sure, Annie, not a problem, but I got to go here pretty quick, anyway." I get up to stretch, put my hat on, and she says what I knew she would.

"Oh now, wait just a minute, mister pro poker player. I know you have a prior commitment to the see the president, but you sure didn't strike me as the type to just cut and run." She's smiling, and there is a twinkle in the eye but there's something else, too.

Ronnie glides over, coming out of nowhere.

"Annie, if he keeps playing you, we're not only gonna be late to the engagement we have, but we'll be dead broke. Not to mention embarrassed all to hell." He made it seem like him and Annie had gone to high school together.

It didn't work this time. Her smile slipped a little, still there, just sagged into a coming sneer.

I step towards her shaking my head slow.

"Annie, if it was up to me I'd sit right here and play you all night. Why hell, I can't think of a more enjoyable time, or how I could be in any more beautiful company." I look sideways over the table. "Sorry, Casey, but I ain't talking about you."

I was overdoing the charm and aw-shucks schmooze because I knew that would get under her skin even more. I throw my hands in the air with mock frustration. "I really should go, though."

Come on, sweetheart, you gonna take that bullshit from me?

Her smile melts away altogether now.

Oh yeah. That's my girl.

"I understand, Cord. You go on ahead now. Your handler there is snapping his fingers at you." She waves around the table at a ring about two or three people deep who are looking on. "It's gotta be tough for you in front of everybody, though. Not making your own decisions, having someone tell you what to do. Even something like this you can't make the decision."

"Annie, look it's—"

"On top of all that, you run into someone like me. Someone that the great and mighty Cord Needham should beat in his sleep, but it just seems like you can't."

There was a soft whistle, and a low hum went around the group watching the game.

"Take her down, Cord." A deep, low voice murmured from somewhere in the small crowd.

A short silence and then another voice snickers, "You mean cards, or the other? Get in line, dude."

A soft chuckle goes around the table.

"All right now, that's enough of that kind of talk." I hold a respectable calming hand up and look around at everyone. My turn to smile now and I glance back to her, taking my hat off with a little flourish. I'm looking at her as if I'm gonna say something like "What am I gonna do with you, young lady?" but then I just shrug my shoulders. "We're all friends here, and this about having a good time. So hey, how can I possibly resist your invitation to stay, darlin'?"

I turn to Ronnie and dramatically motion him to come close. "Call them and tell 'em we're gonna be late for the taping."

Ronnie nods twice, pulls out his cellphone to call no one, and strolls away. He stares at the floor and talks low, just serious as hell.

"So! You do have a pair? So to speak, I mean." Her smile was back, and she brushes softly by me on the way to the ladies' room. "Keep my chair warm, sugar." She smells fresh. Like a spring rain.

I watch her go, and man, everything moves and shifts just right. I don't really know her but then again, I do. It's clear to me that she deserves the hurt I'm going to bitch slap her with. I don't want her money, but I sure want to see that pretty face when she has to get up and leave.

I'll say one thing, she has some money. I don't know who daddy is, but he makes sure the little princess here wants for nothing. She has cashed for chips twice in the last hour. Thirty thousand the first time and now forty this time around.

The pit boss was called over to authorize. It's just a formality, and it happens all the time on a sizable chip buy.

It didn't take her long to come back and I decided to amp it up a little more. "Annie, let's go get us a drink and something to eat, okay? On me. You really don't want to do this."

Dead silence, except the casino noise around us.

"Casey. Help me out here?" I looked up at him with concerned raised eyebrows, but of course I was really hoping that he wouldn't say a damn thing. And he didn't.

"Casey hasn't got anything to do with this, ace. This is between you and I." She doesn't look at me when she speaks, she just keeps sliding the stacks of new chips over in front of her.

The dealer has left the money on the table where she placed it, and now he quickly announced the transaction of forty thousand that had just taken place. Just a matter of policy.

"Annie, look, this is supposed to be a good time here, and we've all had one, so we should just get up and go on our way. I enjoyed this, but I—"

"Play cards."

So, play cards we did. It took me a while because of the table limits on bets, but I got there.

If this would have been a real tournament, no limit game, I'd have run her off the table in a couple of big hands. She was done now, though. A little run of stupid luck earlier, that's all it was.

Lover Boy was already busted out. He's a much better player than her, a dangerous player in fact, but he just didn't have enough money. You got to have it to make it, most of the time. Sure doesn't hurt, anyway.

He has now become her biggest fan and is clearly betting on something else later tonight at this point. He's standing just off of her left shoulder giving my ass the evil eye the whole time.

No one else has sat down to play, and the group watching the game has grown considerably. Quite the little square off for what started out as just an easy-going afternoon game of Hold 'Em.

I was about to stick the knife in and twist it. Along with the money she has spent in the last hour or so, she has to have lost another thirty she had when I first sat down at the table. Rich or not, a hundred or so grand is a lot of money, especially for someone who's not a pro gambler.

So as it turns out, she's like so many other good poker players that know the game pretty well. They know some little tricks they've learned along the way, and they can hold their own with most players they'll run up against. They have guts which you need, but play with gut feels, which you don't need. They always play with too much hope.

What these good poker players don't know or understand is other people. It's why they'll always only be good poker players. Winning high poker, at my level, is more about people than cards or odds.

Anyway, it's her bet, and I'm watching and waiting. I peek three straight times at my hole cards, just for the fuck of it. She knows I'm probably going to see and raise whatever she does.

There is also no indication she was going to dig in that bag for any more money—whatever is left, that is. There would be no more chip buys today.

So, she did what she had to do.

"I'm all in."

She says it with a rueful smile, but her tone is different. A little too extra heavy on the confidence. Not noticeable to most, but just a *little* too much. She also doesn't slide the chip stacks out to the middle this time, she's picking them up and setting them down. Again, barely worth noting, but in poker, everything means something. She is being decisive—and she's also full of shit.

Annie's probably working the same possible straight I am on the flop, although I'm not really working it. I have mine already. Hell, I'm just trying to make it better. Maybe hit a straight flush. To rub it in, I just need a king of hearts on the river.

Even if I don't flush on the straight, I just know she can't have four of a kind, and a hidden boat is next to impossible, too.

"Annie, I tried to let you out of this easy. Tried earlier to open a door for you." I can't help getting a little shitty with her here, but I make it sound like I really hate doing this. "I mean, I have to stay with this hand...I'm in."

She doesn't say anything and stares at me hard. *Pissed? Oh yeah. Dreaming of vengeance that she'll never get a chance at? Oh. Hell. Yeah.*

Her eyes hold something else too, though, like I said before. And it's spooky, makes me nervous, so I do what I always do. I smile at her. And yeah, maybe it's kinda a smirk.

The heat in those beautiful green eyes turns way up now, and it doesn't take a genius to realize that she's probably capable of doing just about anything. She not batshit crazy by any means, but she's a cold-hearted little thing. Very cold.

She's waiting for me to throw my cards face up first, kind of a final fuck you on her part because it really didn't matter.

"Whatcha got there, punkin'?" I say it softly as I'm throwing my straight in the middle of the table. She throws hers too, almost immediately. I know I've won. She knows it too. Me folding had been her only hope to stay alive for another hand.

Annie just keeps staring at me and doesn't even look at the cards. Burning red hot now.

As the crowd whoops it up, she gets up and shoves her chair in. Grabs her bag and throws it over her shoulder. She says something to Lover Boy and starts to storm out. He says something back to her, in her ear over the noise, and she stops. Looks up at him and then looks at me.

He starts coming around the table towards me, but he's watching Ronnie too, twenty feet away.

The dealer burns and turns the river card, but it's just a formality. She had what the little boy shot at of course, and me, well, I hit that royal flush. Talk about icing on the cake.

Everybody all around the game table is pointing at that king of hearts and whooping it up all over again. Wide eyes and shaking heads make it even worse for her. I love it. Her losing is better than me winning.

I'm shaking some old boy's hand, and I feel a hand clamp my upper arm. Hard, strong clamp.

"That was total bullshit, you fuckin' showboat asshole. Proud of yourself?"

The small crowd is quieting down, but I don't think anyone heard him. He was about my size and my age, too, for that matter. I'm also sure I was right earlier. Athletic guy, played some kind of ball. Well, so did I, and fuck him, too. It ain't like he's the fucking Terminator.

I lean in, smile my best Cord Needham smile, and clamp his free arm the same way. It looked like we were old army buddies.

"Hey, I know you don't mean that. Listen, I also know where you're at, pardner." I'm loud now, but oh so understanding and humble. "Believe me, I know what you're feelin'. I been there many times. Hell, just last night!" I said all this even louder so everyone hears me.

Everybody laughs good-naturedly. I nod at Annie and Lover Boy, then touch the brim of my hat. "You're both really good players. Good luck to you."

The small crowd yells and applauds. I come in a little closer and clap him on the arm again. "Now run back over to your new little bitch there. Go upstairs and work that tension out, boy." I say it low and slow, so no one hears me. I'm grinning big.

The crowd noise dies down and starts to break up a little, and Ronnie's closing in fast.

"Fuck you." He shoves me away as he says it.

People heard him.

And gosh, I'm just shocked about this whole situation here.

"Don't do this, Sparky. You don't want any of this." I step in closer to him but hold up my hands showing the crowd of onlookers what a tremendous gentleman I am and what restraint I have.

"You're a coward," he damn near shouts at me. "You just took her money for the hell of it, because you knew you could."

"Now Casey, everyone here knows I tried to leave earlier. Even back when you still had a little money, I tried. And hey, speaking of little money, you got no real skin in this game anyway, Nancy."

He puts a hand on my chest and shoves again, tensing up. It's rock and roll time.

And now, Cord Needham can defend himself honorably as long as I don't go overboard.

Out of the corner of my eye, I see Ronnie, who has just arrived at the scene. "Okay, that's it. What's the problem here? We're all friends here." Ronnie slides in real smooth like only he can. Kind of takes my place in front of Lover Boy.

I nod at Annie on the other side of the table. "I tell you what, hon'. No hard feelings." I stuff some folded over Ben Franklins in Casey's shirt pocket and pat it.

"We don't want your fuckin' money," Casey snarls. He takes the money out of the pocket and throws it at my chest. The bills bounce off and flutter to the floor. "Not that way. I want to play you, superstar. See how you do then. You ain't shit."

Ronnie cuts in again, trying to save the day. "Alright now, look, we really gotta go…and thanks, everyone. Thank you."

The crowd starts to applaud but somebody yells, "Hey, Casey, you better head back to the small tables." Then somebody else shoves that smartass.

"Yeah, we gotta go. Me and Ronnie are running later than a Mexican train. I'm dead serious, though, Lover Boy. Keep that money. You're gonna need it. She's just got to be high maintenance." Big laughs all around on that one.

He lunges for me, but Ronnie is already pushing me away. He's cussing in my ear and shoving me the opposite direction. Somebody else yells something at Casey, somebody else yells something at Annie, and we're on the edge again. There is more shoving and jostling in the crowd, off to my left.

But this is the Magnum, this ain't some boozy strip club, slot machine bar in Carson City. Coming from the right, in a hurry, both over and through people are a bunch of security uniforms. I'm wondering what took them so long.

We're clear, and as we approach the big casino entrance, two big guys in nice suits walk up to us. And I mean big guys.

"You gentlemen doing okay?"

"Sure, sure," Ronnie says, and I notice that he's checking out their name badges.

The one named Michael says, "It's okay sir, we've been sent to stay with you for a bit and assist with anything you might need. You sure you're all right, Mr. Needham?"

I look at them; well, I actually look up at them and smile. "Oh hell, you bet. Never better."

Ronnie shakes his head and rolls his eyes at me.

"I'm thirsty and hungry Ronnie. Like you said earlier, let's go get something good. Knock back a couple or maybe ten Maker's, then get a big, fat-ass, bone-in ribeye about as big as your head."

He looks at me with raised eyebrows. He's always thought I'm hinged a little loose.

I give him a shoulder. "Hey, I can afford it."

Michael holds a hand up graciously. "The Magnum management has already arranged for a private table for you and Mr. Turnbull at the Parisian upstairs. Whatever reservation time you wish. Nothing but the very best up there, as you know. Absolutely no limit on food or drink. Any guests you might have are also welcome. Full comp."

"That's it? That's all you're prepared to offer? I mean this has been very traumatic." I smile at him.

"It's the very least we can do for the reigning WPA Champion and to try to compensate for this...this unfortunate...situation." His voice and polish don't match the outside package.

"Well, I guess." I hook a thumb behind me, "But only if they'll join us at the table."

"No sir, I don't think they'll be making it." The other big guy named "John" grins and smiles at us.

Then we all laugh.

Life is pretty damn good.

SEVEN
Casey

"I don't understand," Babe Parcella said, his voice full of mock confusion. "I mean, I just don't get it."

"Babe—"

"Yeah, shut the fuck up." He smiled, but it was a cold smile. As in Canada cold, which is about how far away I'd like to be right now. Not sitting in this small "hospitality" room off the casino floor. Last time I checked, true hospitality rooms didn't have eyelets for handcuffs welded to the table.

I looked over at Annie. Her expression was flat and cold, but when she glanced my way, I saw a flicker of vulnerability there. Like she still needed me to step up. So I pushed my luck a little.

"It was that Needham guy," I said. "He conned her out of her money and then was an asshole about it, too. The whole thing was his fault."

Babe's smile didn't waver, but it got harder and colder. "Really?"

I nodded. "He should be the one sitting in here instead of us."

"Really?"

"Being a big shot doesn't mean—"

"Really?"

I stopped. Once Babe started in with one-word interruptions, the conversation was over. He'd made up his mind. Of course, I knew he'd made up his mind the minute his goons grabbed up both Annie and I and hauled us into this room. But I had to try. She was watching me.

"You done?" Babe asked.

I nodded.

"Good." He took a deep breath and let out a sigh. I could smell the coffee on his breath, riding under the peppermint Altoids. Or maybe it was Rolaids. Who knew? His job had to be stressful.

Before he could speak, the smartphone on the table in front of him chirped. He glanced down at the screen, tapped it, and read. Then he looked up again.

"First off," he said, holding up his meaty forefinger, "nobody cons anyone at our poker tables. You sit down, you play, you win, you lose, but no one gets conned. If you didn't know who you were playing with, that's on you. If you knew and played anyway, that's on you, too. Our dealer was there, we had the eye in the sky, and there was no cheating whatsoever at that table."

"That's not what I meant."

"I don't give a flying two-fisted fuck what you meant. I'm telling you the way that it *is*. And I shouldn't have to, because you know better."

I didn't have an answer for that. He was right, but what Needham did still had no class to it.

Babe raised another fat finger. "Second off, the man you chested up to was last year's WPA champion."

"I know who he is. And he lost this year, so—"

"So he finished third. And earned more finishing third than you'll win or lose in your entire miserable life. So once again, shut the fuck up. I have to tell you a third time, it gets painful."

I fell silent and leaned back in my chair, waiting for him to finish.

He didn't disappoint. "You also know how it works. Big money and big show gamblers aren't wrong here in Vegas, even when they *are* wrong. And Cord Needham wasn't wrong. He took your money." He paused and frowned at me, and I heard

the unheard accusation—
and after I staked you, too!
—in his voice. He turned to Annie. "And he took a whole lot of yours. But he did it fair and square, and even if he stole it right out of your purse, he's Cord fucking Needham. He may not win the big one this year, but he's still just about the most popular guy on the circuit. And you go and try to *hit* him? In *my* place?"

I didn't answer. My luck had run out, and I didn't want to experience what bad luck meant just now.

Annie didn't say a word, either. In fact, aside from producing her identification when Babe first came in the room, she'd been cool and still and silent the entire time.

"That game does *not* play here at the Magnum," Babe went on. He picked up his smartphone and waved it at us. "What if some asshole had one of these? He gets his camera rolling, and how would that look on YouTube?" He dropped the phone on the table and shook his head. "I ought to ban the both of you for life."

My stomach fell. A lifetime ban probably didn't matter to Annie, but the Mag was top three for me for places to earn. And Babe knew it.

He rubbed his chin thoughtfully, staring at us both. Mostly at Annie, though. I knew he couldn't be immune to whatever it was that she had. But Babe was the consummate professional. Besides, he could land pretty much any woman in town, without a whole lot of work, either.

Then again, Annie wasn't just any woman.

Finally, Babe dropped his hand and turned back to me. "You're gone for thirty days, Case. No exceptions. Don't even come in to use the bathroom or to report a fire or nothing. You get me?"

I nodded, relief washing over me. Thirty days I could do. It would hurt, but I could do it.

He fixed his eyes on Annie. "And I'm going to have to ask you to leave, too. For the same. Thirty days."

Annie smiled coldly. "So much for the upgrade to a suite, then."

Babe shrugged. "You did this, both of you. This isn't me. And I gotta run a tight ship." He pointed at Annie. "My guys will escort you to your room so you can get your things. Your car is already waiting out front."

Annie did not say a word.

Babe turned back to me. "Nicky's waiting out front for you."

"You called Nicky?" I asked, stunned.

Babe stared back at me.

I swallowed and glanced over at Annie. Her expression revealed nothing. I turned back to Babe, and I swore I could see the tiniest of smirks tugging at the corner of his mouth.

You son of a bitch.

Nicely played, I had to admit. Tell Annie about Nicky and probably screw up any chance I had with her. Additional penalty for messing up in his place. And maybe he gets a crack at Annie later. Maybe he reverses giving her the boot.

You cock-blocking son of a bitch.

"Are we done here?" I asked him, surprised at the edge in my voice.

Babe nodded shortly. "I sure hope so."

We rose in unison. Babe handed Annie her ID card. She slipped it into her purse, rummaged around for a second or two, then took out a small fold of money. She held it out to me.

"For your trouble," she said and gave me a look.

What did that look say? Jesus, it said *everything*. Everything I'd ever want to hear.

I took the money and opened my mouth to ask her where she would go now. But the fold felt stiffer than it should have, and her gaze told me things. Instead, I put the money in my pocket and told her, "I'm sorry for the trouble I caused you."

"Yeah," Babe said, "this is sweet and all, but since the only one you should be apologizing to is me, how about we cut this little moment short and get the fuck out of my casino?"

Annie slipped past me, brushing her shoulder against mine. Her fingers trailed lightly and quickly across my hand. Electricity shot through me, fiery and intense. That touch said the same things her eyes did.

Yes, it said. And *later.*

I watched her go, soaking in the after wash of her perfume. A subtle fragrance, but deep. Bold, but mysterious.

I shook my head slightly. Jesus, I sounded like a commercial for the latest scent from some movie star. But shaking my head didn't shake her or the thought. The skin on my hand where she touched was still an ember.

"A wine glass and a woman's ass," Babe said after the door closed behind her.

I turned away from where she'd been. "Huh?"

"The two things that get a man in trouble most in this world. Booze and broads. Or so they say." He smiled, and this one wasn't quite as cold. "'Course, what they don't say is how much fun both can be."

Nicky's maroon Crown Vic was parked in a loading zone just outside the front doors of the Mag. I looked around to see if I could spot Annie before I got into the car, but she was nowhere to be seen.

When I got close, Nicky popped the door lock. Riding around in a locked car seemed paranoid to me, but I guess if you're in her line of work, it's par for the course. I opened the door and got in.

"Jesus fucking Christ," she said, her tone sharp. "You look like shit, Casey."

She didn't look like shit. Usually, she wore business clothes. Suits and such. But even though she was wearing jeans and a white polo shirt that had a gold badge sewn onto the left breast, she still looked good. Hell, she looked hot and professional all at the same time. Every time I saw her, I remembered why it was that I saw her. Not just her looks, either, but there was something else going on, too. Probably structure. That's what Dr. Phil would say, anyway.

She was gorgeous, yeah. But she was no Annie.

"You're a charmer," I replied, pulling my seatbelt on. I knew she wouldn't move the car until I did.

"What the hell?" she asked, motioning toward the casino as she dropped the car into gear and pulled away. "Am I going to get jammed up over this?"

"No."

"Parcella said you got into a fight. Is someone going to be pressing assault charges? Because I can't make something like that go away, Casey."

"Can't or won't?"

She didn't bother looking at me or answering. Can't or won't, same thing either way.

I shrugged. "There's no problem. Just a dust-up, nothing serious." I hoped Babe was wrong about smartphones and YouTube, or she'd find out I was lying.

"Then why'd he call me to come get you? If it was no big deal."

"Is this a formal interrogation? Don't you need to read me my rights or something before I answer any questions?"

She swerved to the curb and slammed on the brakes. I lurched forward, but the seatbelt cinched me in.

"What the fu—"

"Answer my question!" she snapped. "If it's no big deal, why is the head of casino security calling me to pick you up?"

"Easy," I said. "Jesus."

She stared at me, her dark brown eyes hard.

I sighed. "Look, for one, he's booting me out for a month. Calling you puts an exclamation point on that."

"And?"

"And," I said, "you know he's trying to get in good with you so you'll lay off investigating the Mag."

She continued staring at me, but I could see the gears turning. "Why else?"

"Nothing else."

"Bullshit. Don't lie to me, Casey, or I'll fucking dump you right here, curbside."

I've been playing cards professionally for years now. Got that poker face down, like I said. But bluffing Nicky is the hardest thing I've ever tried to do, and I didn't have it down yet. So I gave her another nugget and hoped it was enough.

"It was Cord Needham," I muttered, looking away.

"Cord Nee—" she stopped. "You got in a fight with a circuit player?"

"It wasn't a fight, just a disagreement."

"Over what?"

"Over he's a dick."

"They're all dicks. What was it about?"

I shook my head. "Stupid shit. Okay? I'm sorry. Like I said, Babe only called you because he wants to make points."

She thought about it a few moments longer. I knew what she was grinding on, and she finally said it. "If he wants me to lay off, there must be something there."

I saw the opening, and I almost didn't take it. That would've been a nice way to say fuck you to Babe. Problem is, he'd never hear it and, in the end, it would be me that took the brunt. So I did the right thing for both of us.

"There's nothing there," I said.

Her eyes narrowed. "How would you know?"

"I'm in the place all the time. And you know I can read people. There's nothing going on in the Mag that's any different than every other casino on the Strip. So unless you want to close down all of—"

"Then why is he trying to cozy up?"

"Because a cop poking around gives the appearance that something is wrong. And here in Vegas, appearance is everything. That's why he tossed me. Can't have local riff-raff bothering the whales or the showmen, can we?"

She considered what I said. After a few seconds, she put the car back into gear and pulled into traffic.

We drove in silence for a while. I watched her out of my peripheral vision. The police radio chirped and squawked, but she didn't seem to pay attention. I knew she heard every word, though. She was most definitely and completely in work mode.

"What's today?" I asked.

"The seventh."

"No, the day. Of the week."

She glanced over. "Are you fucking kidding me?"

"It's not Friday, right?" I motioned toward her clothes. "I'm just wondering why you're dressed for casual Friday, is all."

She scowled. "Cute."

I tried to smile disarmingly, but she was having none of it.

"It's not casual Friday, wise-ass. It's my day off, is what it is. And I got called out on a homicide. You call me out on my day off, you get casual. I might've had time to dress nicer, but I got another call right about the time I was standing in front of my closet. Know what that call was about?"

I knew. Babe.

"Sorry," I murmured.

"Sorry? Oh, you're sorry?"

"I am."

"Yeah? For what?"

"Making you late to your homicide scene."

"Fuck you, Casey."

"You know, if all you were going to do was break my balls, why didn't you tell Babe to go to hell? Don't even come for me. Save us both the hassle."

"Because, smart guy, he said it was either I pick you up or he calls patrol. You like the jail experience?"

"Not particularly," I said, though it figured it was six-five and pick 'em at the moment between her shit and jail.

"Then you got me."

We drove for a while longer. I couldn't figure out where she was headed, but I could tell she wasn't entertaining any questions. Her thin fingers were wrapped around the steering wheel hard enough to make the knuckles whiten. Those white knobs stood out against the cocoa brown of her skin. After a while, she repeated quietly, "It was my day off."

Oh. Shit.

"I'm sorry," I answered, my voice softer, too.

"It's not like I get a lot of them." Her tone was a little hurt. "You could've come around. Spent some time."

I almost answered that it wasn't like I could keep track of when she had time off. It wasn't like she worked a normal schedule, or like her days off didn't get canceled three times out of five. Right now was a case in point. But she didn't want to hear that.

"I'm sorry," I repeated. "You could've called. Or texted me."

"I shouldn't have to," she said, her voice still in that hurt tone.

There was no arguing that point. Not with a woman. And cop or not, hard-ass Chicago girl or not, Lieutenant Nicky Raines was definitely still a woman.

I fell on my sword. "You're right. I should've checked in. I'm sorry. Really."

She took a deep breath and let it out. "Yeah, I know, Casey. You're always sorry."

I didn't have an answer for that one. And that had nothing to do with her being a woman, either.

We drove five more minutes and by then we were on the outskirts of the city. I rubbed my eyes, glanced around, and finally asked, "Where are we going?"

"To the scene. I don't have time to drop you. I'm already late."

I nodded and said nothing. It wasn't like Nicky and I were a secret exactly, but I also knew she wasn't taking out billboard space about it. I was an exposure for her if I ever got into some kind of trouble. Like the kind I was in with the Swede, and now with Babe, too. It was dangerous for me, but it was dangerous for her as well. At best, it could hurt her chances at making captain. At worst, it was an Internal Affairs beef that got her demoted or fired.

And yet, she was still with me. Picking me up from trouble I was in. And taking me with her to a homicide scene.

I didn't quite know what to make of that.

We cruised along for another ten minutes, and then she took a side road off the main county two-lane. I remembered the old saying about Vegas from back in the days when it all got started. About there being lots of holes getting dug out in the desert. I wondered if they were even bothering with the holes anymore.

Nicky slowed. A dirt road ahead was marked with a police cruiser. A uniformed officer waved her to the right, and she took it. A half mile later, we rolled up to what looked like an outdoor rock festival parking lot, complete with police cars, fire trucks, an ambulance, and a couple of news vans.

"Wait here," Nicky said, putting the car into park.

"I'm not sitting in the car like some ten-year-old whose mommy is going into the store to pick up milk," I said.

"Casey, I gotta work now. Okay? So don't give me any of your shit."

"I'll stay out of the way."

She didn't reply but shut off the car and pulled out the key. That was answer enough. No way would she expect me to stay in the car without the air conditioning.

I got out of the car and trailed after her. She walked with a confident stride. Her big, gold lieutenant's badge gleamed in the sun, and the gun on her hip looked like something Dirty Harry would carry. I tried to remember if it was a .40 or a .45 but couldn't. Not that it mattered. It just looked big because she wasn't. Besides, she could put three shots inside a dime from a hundred yards. Or something like that. I didn't know guns, but I gathered her shooting accuracy was the equivalent of being able to catch the outside corner of the plate, breaking away, every time.

I slowed down as we neared the yellow tape. Nicky kept right on walking, and the uniform cop lifted the tape for her, giving her a respectful nod. Nicky nodded back but didn't break stride. She headed toward the huddle of cops near a dried-out tree without looking back.

I took the opportunity to take the money Annie had given me out of my pocket. I was right about the stiffness. She'd wrapped five one-hundred-dollar bills around a plain white business card. It was expensive cardstock, embossed with gold lettering. Just a single "A" and a telephone number. I didn't recognize the area code.

I smiled to myself. I put the business card in my left pants pocket and slid the cash into my right. Even though the five bills meant a little stake money, I felt like the card in my left pocket was the real treasure.

I walked up to the edge of the crime scene tape and scanned until I found Nicky. She was standing next to a cop in a suit. Detective, probably. He stepped away from the group and waved for her to follow him. When she moved, there was a break in the gaggle around the body, and I got a look inside the circle. Then, like a single being, the group crowded in and blocked my view.

It was just a flash, but it was enough.

My stomach fell, then heaved.

I leaned over, put my hands on my knees and threw up at the patrolmen's feet.

"Shit!" the cop said, stepping back to avoid the spray.

"I'm sorry," I grunted and turned away.

Yeah. I'm always sorry.

The rest of the uniform cops left me alone, shooting me looks filled with suspicion and disgust. Some ambulance driver was concerned enough to check on me, but I told him I was feeling better. He gave me a bottle of water. I sat on the bumper of Nicky's car, sipping and spitting until the taste was mostly out of my mouth. Then I guzzled the rest and stared at the group huddled by the tree in the distance.

I tried to convince myself I hadn't seen what I saw, but I knew I had. The guy up there must've been lying on his back, because his toes were pointing up in the air. I could see the bottom half of his legs, and they were crossed at the ankle. He wore a pair of black and white checkered shoes.

That's what I saw. And I couldn't deny it.

So next I told myself that maybe they were Vans or boat shoes or whatever they call 'em. But that was crap, too, and I knew it. Those were dress shoes and they tapered almost to a point. And even out here in the dirty desert, the sun glinted off of them, so I knew they'd been shined recently.

Just like they were shined every day. I knew that, too. Because I knew who wore those shoes. And it was just one guy. Who wears checkered shoes, for Christ's sake?

Grady Burns, that's who.

He was a player. Old-school. Liked to play the five-card game. Draw or stud. Always said that was real poker, unlike Hold 'Em, which he complained was for people who grew up on video games. Oh, he played Hold 'Em and was good enough at it. Had to, really, because that was where everybody's money was these days. But he bitched about it every time.

I guessed his bitching days were finished. Unless someone stole his ugly-ass shoes and then got clipped and dumped in the desert while wearing them.

I stood watching everybody up by the tree as they milled around. Nicky didn't look my way once. She just directed activities. One man sketched. Another man took pictures. Several were on the phone.

The thing was, I knew something probably none of them did. Grady and I had something in common. We were both into it deep to the Swede. I didn't know what his numbers were, but they couldn't have been much bigger than mine. And he'd been losing a lot lately, and then he started chasing it, which is always a losing proposition.

Grady was sixty-eight years old. Maybe sixty-nine. I couldn't remember. I just recalled that it'd been three or four years ago when he started making jokes about being staked the first of every month by Uncle Sam. He even flashed his Social Security check at the table one time, his thumb carefully over the dollar figure and snatching it back before anyone had time to read the deposit amount where it was spelled out.

Sixty-eight years old.

Jesus.

I let out a wavering breath. The taste of bile was still in my mouth, and I could feel the acid on my teeth. I wished for more water.

Grady was a cool, old-school gambler. He was a quiet institution to those of us in the game. But he owed the Swede. And by whacking him and not bothering to dig a hole, the Swede was making a statement. He was saying that nothing mattered. Not who you were, not who you knew, not your station in life, not your age.

Nothing.

I needed some money.

And fast.

EIGHT
Cord

The elevator stops, and two real pretty girls step in at the twenty-first floor. Both of them dressed to the nines.

I mean, this is Vegas, for cryin' out loud. There is a fine-lookin' girl or woman everywhere you turn. Hell, you can't take ten steps without running into one. But damn, I can't stop thinking about little Annie back there at the table.

She was a little hottie, no doubt, but it was more than that. There was also a feeling of "proceed with caution" and a level of mystery thing she had going on just under the surface.

It's all I can think about on this elevator as we go up. I'd usually be talkin' it up right now with these two that just got on, but I don't.

The elevator chimes softly, and they get off on the twenty-sixth floor, long hair, longer legs, and high heels a-clicking. The shorter one of the two shoots me a look and a grin as they go. I tip my hat out of habit only. The doors swish shut.

"Thanks a lot, asshole. I mean, you know, don't worry about me. I ain't proud, I'da taken whichever one you didn't just then." Ronnie shakes his head at me in disgust, then grins. "You not feeling good or what?"

"Hey, I'm saving myself for my true love Annie downstairs." I put my hand over my heart and tap it.

Ronnie lets out a big laugh on that one, and our two apes,

Michael and John, both have a chuckle, too.

Even though it was only about five or so, we had taken the dinner offer up right away because Ronnie and I were both starved. We were dressed okay too, so what the hell. I needed a few pops before dinner anyway.

The Parisian is all the way up on the top floor of the Magnum, and the doors finally open. As we approach, it's pretty damned impressive. Two huge, white pillars frame the entryway.

Inside, the place has very low lighting, and it's just dripping with gold and polished-brass opulence. Our two boys lead us in past the gorgeous hostess, who smiles and steps aside, waving us through like she's Vanna White on Wheel of Fortune or some shit. We make our way toward a back, corner table with one helluva view of the city. No other tables have anybody at them yet. This is like lunchtime in Vegas.

"Mr. Needham, I trust this is a suitable table?" Michael says. Then he pushes his earpiece in a little better and cocks his head for a second.

"Well hell, I would hope so. Yes, absolutely."

A chair is pulled out for me by John, and then one for Ronnie too.

"You'll be well taken care of by the maître de and our entire dining staff. Anything at all you'd like tonight, compliments of the Magnum." Michael pauses for effect, clasps his hands in front of him, then spreads them. "No limits—just like the card game you play so well."

"Not always, I don't. I wish I was playin' that little Frenchman later tonight." I gaze out the huge wall of glass that lines the entire restaurant. I'm sure it looks like I'm disappointed about that and thinking about René Gaust.

"Well sir, is there anything else we can do for you before we excuse ourselves and let you dine?"

"Michael, I honestly don't know what that could possibly be," Ronnie says as he stands and shakes hands with both of them.

He palms them both some cash. "You guys have been tremendous, and be sure to pass along our sincere thanks to the manager."

"Yes, thanks, guys. Y'all been great." I stand up and shake their hands, too. "Magnum is hands down the best hotel casino in Vegas. You can tell the manager that I said that."

"Very much appreciated, Mr. Needham." He nods at Ronnie. "Mr. Turnbull."

John turns to go, too, waves and says, "Have a good evening, gentlemen."

Ronnie sits down, but I remain standing up, struck with an idea. More of a thought, really. It was stupid and wild-assed, but nobody ever accused me of being brilliant.

I hold up a hand. "Hey, John, Michael, hold up."

"Yessir?" Michael says, returning to the table.

"There is one request I have, but I really need your help with this one."

I could feel Ronnie staring at me, and I smile down at him. His chin flops down to his chest dramatically. He knew. The little bastard just knew what I was going to say. I swear he can read my mind like no other.

"No, Cord..." Ronnie mutters.

"Michael, I want to invite someone up here to dinner, but I don't know how to get a hold of her."

"Cord, don't do this."

"Of course, Mr. Needham." Michael was trying to look at me but grinning uneasily down at Ronnie, too.

"Annie. It's Annie. I want to invite her to have dinner with us here."

"Mr. Needham, I don't think that..." He looks at John, and John stares wide-eyed back at Michael.

"Just her, though." I can't get the grin off my face. I just love shit like this. "Without that grunt watchdog she had with him, I mean."

"Unfortunately..." Michael begins.

"Call whoever you have to, Michael. I'll take full responsibility, and it'll be fine. Let me talk to your boss if that will help.

"Mr. Needham, I'm almost positive she's no longer on the premises."

I grin even bigger and look at my watch.

"It's been less than a half hour since our little dust-up downstairs. No woman on earth would be packed and gone by now."

"Okay, Mr. Needham, I'll make a quick call to see if anything can be done." He's smiling and all, but it's strained.

Walking to the windows about twenty feet away, he pulls a cell phone out and makes a call. It doesn't take long for him to get an answer, and he comes back to our table after only a minute or so.

"Well, Mr. Needham, my supervisor, the Head of Security here at The Magnum, told me she has been told to leave the hotel premises after what happened."

"Now, hold on, Mike. Let me talk to your boss. I didn't want..."

He smiles at me and holds up an index finger.

"However, our Head of Security is positive that she has not checked out yet, and he said if that's what you really want, he'll handle it himself."

"I'll take full responsibility. It'll be fine if that turd is not here."

"Believe me, Mr. Needham, there won't be any further problems with him. He won't be back for a long time."

"Well, great. And hey, we're in no hurry at all here to eat dinner. Ronnie and I will just sit back have a few drinks. You tell him that, okay?"

Ronnie finishes his third drink and clunks the glass down hard on purpose. "You're such an ass sometimes."

"Thanks, pardner." I give him a sly grin and twirl what's left of my drink around.

"All right, man, I'll do it. But I ain't leavin' until I know she will be cool. Hell, until I know *you'll* be cool."

"Hey, look where we're at," I look around the room. "We'll be fine, she'll be fine. This will be the best damn dinner she's ever had. Relax, I'll be a charming bastard."

"Oh, shee-it."

Ronnie's gaze goes from over my shoulder to casually looking out the window as if he was admiring dusk and the brightening city night lights outside. "They're coming. So, be nice."

"Room service has got to be good here, man."

"Mr. Needham?"

I turn slightly and look up at a fucking suited gorilla. A huge beefy hand reached out to me.

I stand up and shake it. "Yessir, that's me."

I can barely see her with his bulk, but she's behind him all right, arms crossed shyly in front of her. She's smiling at me, a real smile and damn, she looks like a million frickin' bucks. I mean, really.

"A pleasure, Mr. Needham. I'm Babe Parcella, Head of Security for Magnum Enterprises. I have someone here whom you know from a prior engagement." He smiles at me and then her, bringing her gently forward with one big tree trunk of an arm.

She steps forward. I take off my hat and quickly set it on the table.

I look at her and say, "Ms. Kozak, thanks for accepting my invitation."

"Thanks for extending it." Her voice is soft and demure.

We stare at each other for a moment.

Ronnie clears his throat.

"Well, listen, folks," Parcella says, "I'm going to get going here, and I couldn't be happier for how this turned out."

I tear my eyes away from her. "Mr. Parcella, great to meet you, and before I leave here in a few days, I'm gonna talk to the general manager of this place. By the time I'm done talking to him, you'll be managing a casino yourself. Hell of a job today by you and your people."

He holds up a palm that looks like a third baseman's glove. "Mr. Needham, it's the least we can do."

Annie suddenly, impulsively turns now and hugs Parcella. The hug lasts a while.

She's looking at me though as she's hugging him. There is that certain something dancing in her beautiful eyes. She's smiling but...

I can't even tell you what she's wearing because it doesn't matter.

I should leave right now.

But I don't and won't.

Man, can she hold a room.

NINE
Casey

After she finished up at the murder scene, Nicky was quiet on the drive back into the city. I figured it was even up whether she was going to drop me off without a word or take me back to her apartment and rock me. I never knew which way she was going to go, or what exactly pushed her one direction or the other. We never talked about what she saw on the job.

The truth was, right about now, I wasn't sure which outcome I was hoping for. But where Nicky was concerned, what I wanted didn't really matter, anyway.

She swung a right on Fig and that told me what I needed to know. A few minutes later, she pulled up in front of my apartment complex.

I hesitated, even though I wanted to get out. Nicky looked over at me, giving me her cool cop stare. She probably thought it was impassive, like my poker face, but it wasn't. There was brooding aggression and hate hiding under that mask. I always wondered if she knew what a bitch she looked like with that expression on her face.

I wasn't about to tell her.

"What?" she asked, testily.

I shook my head. "Nothing. I just wanted to say I'm sorry."

She didn't answer.

"About not calling you on your day off," I added. "And you

getting called out, too."

She shrugged. "Call-out pay. Big bucks. Ka-ching." There was no joy in her voice. "Not like I'll ever get a chance to spend any of it, though, you know?"

Yeah, I knew. Tough problem to have. Not like I couldn't use some of it, but there was no way I could ask her.

"Well, sorry." I waited another moment, then pulled the door handle and got out. Nicky pulled away as soon as I closed the car door. Her tires chirped, and she sped off like a bat out of hell.

Jesus, when do cops ever *not* drive fast?

Inside my apartment, I slapped together a sandwich out of what I could salvage from the refrigerator. I guzzled one of the two beers left in there, too, then stood in my tiny kitchen, sipping the last one.

I took the five hundred out of my pocket and dropped it on the counter. Then I pulled out the elegant white card and stared at it.

A.

For Annie, of course.

Only "Annie" didn't quite fit her. I wondered what it was short for. Andrea? Angelica? Or something more exotic, like Anastasia?

Whatever it was, "Annie" was for when she was slumming, which was definitely what she was doing here in Vegas.

I sipped the Red Stripe and continued staring at the card. I decided I should call her.

But not yet. I needed to be fresher. On my game. She wasn't like every other woman. I couldn't afford to fuck it up. This was going to take more than the standard Casey Brunnell charm.

I finished off the bottle, set it on the counter, and shuffled down the short hall to the bedroom. I flopped onto the bed, intending to sleep a couple of hours, just a refresher nap, but once I closed my eyes, I'd lost all of the night.

QUEEN OF DIAMONDS

The next morning, I woke late. The sun came through a break in the curtains and slashed across my pillow and into my face. Even with the AC on, that sun was still hot.

I staggered out of bed and into the shower. Once I felt slightly human, I fished around for some clean clothes. Dressed, I went out into the kitchen. My stake money and her card were still there, waiting patiently for me.

Chase the cards or chase the girl?

Hell, it wasn't even a question.

I drove down to an off-strip diner, where the prices actually are what people think Vegas prices should be. I sucked down two cups of coffee with my eggs and bacon, and then I was ready.

Payphones aren't as plentiful in this cell phone age. I kept thinking I should get a cell, but then the question always comes up. Who would I call? I'm not close with any of my family, and they're few enough of them, anyway. So, who? Nicky? The Swede? I stuck with the hard line in the apartment and, while I could still get them, payphones.

She picked up on the second ring. "Hello?"

"Hey, uh, this is Casey. From the card game yesterday?"

"Casey. Of course. I'm glad you called, Casey."

I liked the sound of my name coming from her lips. "I was wondering if maybe you'd like to get some breakfast?"

"It's after one."

"Lunch, then."

"I already ate."

"Oh." I was still thinking about those lips and about the electric thrill of her touch. "Well..."

"But I'd really like to see you, Casey. Maybe you can help me with something."

"Sure."

"Tell me where you are."

I gave her the address.

"Be there in fifteen minutes."

I stood at the payphone and waited, feeling excited and nervous at the same time. When was the last time I'd been this crazy over a woman? Not since before I started playing Single A. Before the baseball draft, when the women became all too available and perfectly meaningless. Before that had been hormones more than anything else. This was…different.

I waited dutifully, and she was on time. She pulled up in a red convertible. Her hair was pulled back in a simple, elegant ponytail. She looked over at me, pulled her glasses down on her nose, and said, "You want a ride, sailor?"

I did.

We drove for a few minutes without a word. It was strangely reminiscent of my last ride with Nicky. I pushed thoughts of her out of my mind. It wasn't like we were married, and even if we were, so what?

"They treat you all right after I left?" I asked her.

She smirked. "They were patient enough while I got my things together. Then they walked me out to my car and said adios, fuck you very much."

I smiled. "I got the same."

"Of course. How dare we presume to call out royalty?"

I smiled bigger. She had some grit, this one.

"Where are you staying now?" I asked.

"The Riviera."

I raised my eyebrows. The Riv was nice enough, but it was an older hotel and casino, not one of the newer and fancier themed hotels. And it was at the end of the strip. But maybe that was the point.

"I don't want to bump into that asshole again," she explained. "At least, not until I choose to."

"He'll probably leave town soon."

"He better not leave with my money."

"It's his money now."

"No," she said resolutely. "It's mine."

"Well, you're right about the digs," I told her. "He's not likely to be hanging out at the Riv. Too many newer and fancier places where he can rub elbows with the socialites and get comped everything."

"I figured. I also didn't want to be under the nose of the other one. The big security guy."

"Babe?" I shook my head. "You'll have to go further than the Riviera if you want to fly under his radar. These security heads all have each other's backs. If he puts the word out, he'll hear back."

"Oh well. Just as long as I don't run into Mr. Aw Shucks until I'm ready."

I smiled at that. Needham did pour on the good ol' boy routine a bit thick. "Until you're ready?"

She nodded. "Yeah. I'm going to beat his ass at poker and take my money back, along with a good chunk of his."

She said it as if it were the most natural thing in the world. She was going to beat one of the country's best heads-up players. Oh, but not until she was *ready*.

Her confidence was somehow contagious, and so I wasn't even surprised at her words. Instead, I asked, "When will you be ready?"

"Soon. But I need money first. That's where you can maybe help me, Casey."

"Money? I don't have any."

She smiled. "I know. I saw you lose it."

I felt a moment of stung pride.

Before I could respond, she continued. "I don't have enough money on hand to get him interested in a game or to beat him. I figure I need three or four hundred thousand for that. Does that sound right to you?"

I blinked. That was more than twice what I owed the Swede. Maybe she could—

"Casey?"

"Uh, yeah. At least three hundred kay. Four is better."

She nodded. "I thought so. The thing is, I don't have that kind of cash. But I have some diamonds. Beautiful, unique ones. I need to sell them. Pawn them, really, because after I take back my money and some of that asshole's money, I want to be able to get my diamonds back, too."

I blinked again. I wondered what my poker face was telling her right now.

"Do you know someone who can do that?" she asked. "Pawn my diamonds?"

And then I smiled slowly. "It just so happens I do."

She smiled back, and it was like a bittersweet knife slashed across my chest. Jesus, what was it with this siren?

"Well, then," she said, "lead on."

Perry sat at his desk in the jewelry store, staring at an opal through his jeweler's glass. I'd never seen a jeweler that interested in an opal, but if Perry was looking, there was a profit in it somewhere.

When he saw me, he sighed. "Jeez, I told you a year ago, Casey. The whole ring is gone. Stones got pulled, the metal scrapped. I'm sorry, but I gave you plenty of time."

I shook my head. "Forget about the ring."

"What ring?" Annie asked, coming up from behind me and shooting him a smile.

Perry noticed her and stared. "Uh, he sold me, I mean, he pawned his championship ring. I held onto it for a while, but—"

"Championship?" She took my hand. "What sort of championship?"

"Baseball," I said. "Double A champs."

"You were a baseball player?" She said it in a breathless voice, almost reverent. I didn't know if it was real or for Perry's benefit, but it felt good either way.

"Yeah."

"What position did you play?"

"Catcher."

"And you won the championship?"

"*A* championship," I corrected. "Double A, my last year. They gave us rings."

"Why'd you quit playing?"

"Knee injury."

She gave me a slightly sad look, then glanced over at Perry. "It's too bad about his ring," she said, her tone slightly reproving.

I couldn't see the tactical wisdom in reprimanding the guy who you were about to ask for money, but goddamned if Perry didn't get flustered. "Well, like I said, I hung onto it for a long while, and—"

"It wasn't that valuable," I said. "Not in terms of stones or metal, and not in memories, either." I stared at Annie. "That was a lifetime ago. I'm more interested in the present."

"Then let's get to it," she said, releasing my hand and turning her attention to Perry. "I have some diamonds. They're worth between one point two and one point four million dollars. I want to pawn them with you for four hundred forty thousand for thirty days. If I buy them back, I'll pay four seventy-five. That's thirty-five thousand back on your money. If I don't redeem them, you can keep the diamonds, sell them yourself and pocket the million plus. What do you say?"

Perry blinked. What could he say?

The transaction went rather quickly. Perry examined the huge diamond earrings. His bearings seeming to return as he found himself back in his element. After a careful inspection, he pronounced them excellent quality and stored them in a felt box. Then he drew up a loan slip, which he and Annie both signed. He wrote Annie a check, and we left.

Annie drove straight to a National Savings bank and cashed

the check. Once we were back in the car, she peeled off forty thousand dollars and handed it to me.

"What's this?" I asked, flabbergasted.

"What? You weren't hoping I'd give you some money?"

I stammered out a nonsensical answer.

She laughed. "Relax. It's your cut."

"My cut?"

"Finder's fee. You found Perry. That's worth something. I figure ten percent."

"You could have found Perry," I said. "I don't deserve forty thousand dollars for—"

"No, I couldn't have found Perry," she interrupted. "Not right away. I might have found someone, but it might not be a guy who was willing to accept my terms and not get suspicious."

"I'm sure he's suspicious," I said. "He just sees too much money in this to let suspicion get in his way."

"See?" she said. "That's what I mean. You knew that about him. That's why you took me to him and not to anyone else."

I thought about that. She might be right.

We drove in silence for a few minutes. I was feeling pretty good. My newly enlarged stake just bumped me to some of the bigger tables where I could rape and pillage the weekend Richie Rich types. Maybe I'd win enough to keep the Swede at bay.

"Now what?" I finally asked her.

"Now I get good at poker," she said. "I need to read about it and watch it. That's how I learn."

"So you can beat Needham."

"That's right."

I didn't answer.

"Maybe you can help me with that, too," she said, her voice softer than I'd heard it since we met. "I could use a coach."

A coach. I remembered how it was the kiss of death for a player when the manager started talking about a transition to coaching. It meant your playing days were over, at least as far as that manager was concerned.

"I'm no coach," I said, without really thinking about it.

"A mentor, then," she replied, her voice still soft. "Or...a friend?"

I swallowed, said nothing, and nodded.

We drove the rest of the way without a word.

Her room at the Riviera was as nice as they came at that hotel. It could have been a cave in Pakistan, though, and I don't think I would have noticed.

We were barely in the door, and she was kissing me. I've kissed a ton of women in my time, but none of them kissed like this one. Some kissed like they were hungry, even ravenous. Some kissed lazy. Some had tight, pinched lips. She was altogether different. She kissed me with a kind of fiery patience that seemed to savor every moment but yearn for longer and more at the same time.

After that first long kiss next to the door, the rest was a wet, wonderful blur.

Sometime later, we lay together on the bed, wrapped up in each other's silence. She put her head on my chest and I stroked her hair, only half awake. We lay there for a long while.

"I meant what I said," she whispered.

"Huh?" I startled from the edge of sleep.

"About you being my mentor. I meant it."

"Uh-huh."

"And my friend," she whispered even more softly.

I smiled. She looked up at me and smiled back. Suddenly, I wasn't sleepy anymore. She slid up to my face, kissed me, and we got lost again.

TEN
Cord

"Cord?"

"…Yup, right here…right, Cord speakin'."

Ronnie, least I'm pretty sure it's Ronnie, doesn't say anything more at first. There is just a heavy sigh on the other end.

"Okay, hello, Ronnie? Well…listen, you wanna have some uh…" As I'm talking, I'm squinting at the clock on the nightstand. Red blurred numbers. I put my cellphone in front of my face, try to focus on that. No luck. I'm legally blind. "You wanna have a late breakfast?"

"Shit, son, it's almost three in the afternoon." He isn't pissed off, just has that exasperated father-son thing going on. Even though he's a grand total of one year older than me. "This is like the tenth call I've made or some shit."

"Okay, all right…just relax, would ya? Damn."

"I honestly thought the little darlin' either killed you or loved you to death. She gone yet?"

"She who? Wait, what'd you say?"

"You heard me. I said, is she gone yet?"

I actually glance over next to me to see if she *is* there. I still gotta be about three quarters in the tank.

"You talkin' about, um, Annie?"

"Um, yeah."

There is another pause, and my brain just stalls out. I turn the key to start it and nothing happens. I'm doing the pleasant, slow, fade away.

"Cord? Cord? Hey, listen, this phone call thing won't work too good unless you actually talk."

"Yeah, yeah, I'm right there, man." I slowly rise again, out of the ashes.

"When I left you two at the restaurant, it looked as if you were going to have each other for dessert. I mean, like right there. On the table."

"Oh man, I feel like dog shit."

"And hell, I left early. Before the appetizers even got there."

"Yeah, well, we kinda clicked."

"*Clicked?* And then later at the final, with Gaust and Larry? You two walk in the room and the fuckin' game almost stopped." He chuckles then, and it brings a smile to my face. "I think they went to a commercial. Frenchy was really pissed."

"I remember Gaust winning, but it's hazy, I'll tell you that. I'm glad you can fill in the other details."

He laughed again. "They kept panning the crowd with the camera. I can always tell with you. You looked good, weren't stumbling around, smiling, shaking hands, and kissing babies… but you were drunk on your ass."

"You and I talked at the game?"

There is some shuffling around, and I hear him tell somebody just to keep the change.

"Hey, listen, girlfriend." His voice is high and even more southern now. "I'd love to keep talking about this on the phone while you do your nails, but I'm coming up to your room…unless she's there."

"She ain't here, asshole. If she was, you'd still be trying to call me. Hey, listen, give me a few minutes…hello? Ronnie?" I throw my cell on the bed and then pick up the room phone with a shaky hand.

I punch seven for room service, and it is like a panicked nine-one-one call for me. Even told them to please hurry.

Before I know it, Ronnie is knocking at the door. After fumbling with the two different locks for a minute, I open the door and he looks at me with raised eyebrows. He shakes his head slowly.

"Lord have mercy. Did you order coffee or an exorcism?"

"Coffee. A fuckin' pony keg of it. And one of everything on the menu. Breakfast and lunch." I grin at him and he winces, then shuts his eyes.

"Don't grin again. You looked just like Nicholson in *The Shining*."

"I'm taking a shower."

"Hurry. I want details from last night."

"Bullshit." He's grinning big.

"Serious." I slam another forkful of eggs and then follow that up with a big bite of an English muffin.

"You have got to be kidding me. That girl is not some dainty little unpicked flower." He's shaking his head no and grinning like a fool.

"Easy what you say about my true love. And hell, Ron-bo, I'm not exactly an eagle scout, either." I slug the rest of my coffee down. I'm starting to come back to life. Starting to.

"You're telling me you didn't get there?"

"No, sir. I mean, yessir, that's what I'm sayin'. Swear."

"Well, I'll be damned. I'da bet what Frenchy won last night on that. I wanted to hear all about it, you asshole. And now, you got nothing for me."

"I'll tell you this, though, Sparky…" I finish spreading blackberry jam on another muffin and motion it as an offering to Ronnie.

He holds up his hands.

"You want any of this Ronnie? Shit, just dig in, man."

"I ate already…plus, I don't think I'm fast enough with the fork." He sips his coffee, gets up, and walks to the window.

"Anyway, I'll tell you this, Ronnie…that was the hottest non-sex I've ever had in my life. We were leaning against my door…" I point over to it and grin, "doing everything but making a baby. If someone would have been in the hallway, they'd a called security all over again. Hell, they'd called a S.W.A.T. team. It was a mutual sexual assault."

Ronnie turns from the window and looks at me quizzically. "Well, damn."

"Damn, is right."

"So why, what was the deal? Saving herself for marriage or what? Though it's probably a little too late for that…" He laughed, but I didn't. He noticed.

"Do you know how different that was, bud? How difficult that was?"

"No doubt, it doesn't happen to you…or her…very often." He shrugs. "But, so what? What the hell did that accomplish, except build up one helluva lot of frustration?"

I get up, stretch, and burp like a death row convict after his last meal. Then I burp again. It's a rip-roaring belch, louder than the first time.

"Man, I needed that."

"Last night you mean?"

"No asshole, that food, that burp…and this, of course." I pour another steaming cup of my own version of heroin.

"So, you *really* like her, right? She's different than the rest, right?" He's smirking at me.

"Look, Ronnie, I know what you're thinking. I'm a dumbass who's getting taken for a ride. She's playing me like a fiddle. I know that's what you're thinking, but you're wrong."

He turns back to look at the sweltering day out there. Blazing sun, bluer-than-blue sky, and not the smallest puff of a cloud. "You're a big boy, and you're sure as hell no dumbass…but I just don't believe in love anymore. Not that kind, anyway."

"You know, bud, I haven't had a night like that for a long,

long time. Not since when Laura and I were kids." It's like somebody else is talking right now, and I can barely believe what I'm saying. "Hell. I just haven't felt like that, period. Maybe ever."

He stares at me, looks away, and then stares at me again. "You sound like a love-struck senior in high school."

"I know, sounds crazy, right? Especially when you think about how we met. That didn't exactly start out great, huh?"

"Cord...man...just take a little step back. Take your foot off the gas a bit, that's all I'm sayin'."

"Oh hey, it's cool. That's exactly what she said, too." I walk over and get my cell phone, checking numbers and calls. "We're gonna do something tomorrow. She wants us to slow down and play the thing out a little. See if there's really something there."

I look out the wall of glass now, too. She's all I can think of. Since Ronnie has been here, and as I keep sobering up, I'm remembering how right it all really was last night. And it was definitely *right*. I actually cared about what she had to say. I liked being with her, around her. I remember how I didn't want dinner to end.

Ronnie just keeps staring at me.

"Hey, I'm not saying that the sex attraction thing isn't there. That's pretty damn obvious, but there is something else there, too. Trust me. And it wasn't the booze, either."

He grins at me, but it's a careful, cautious one. "Like I said, you're a big boy, pard. You don't have to explain nothing to me."

"We go way, wayyy the hell back, Ronnie. It matters to me what you think."

Ronnie sets his coffee cup down, points at me, and winks. "Likewise, and you know that."

I've said it before, and I'll say it again, Ronnie is the glue that holds this whole thing together. Holds me together.

He takes his phone out and checks it quickly. "Alright, soooo, let's meet up downstairs in what, an hour or so? We'll talk to the Association boys about Atlantic City, thank the Magnum and Tournament people, all that happy shit."

"All right, son. Sounds good."

"What time you seein' Annie tonight?"

"You mean tomorrow night. I told you, I'm seeing her tomorrow night."

"No, I meant tonight. Hell, Cord, our flight out is tomorrow night at six. You need to see her tonight. Then we need to head to Atlantic City."

"She's having dinner with her brother tonight. He's in town for business, but just for today."

"So, how's this gonna work?"

"Look, I didn't know when our flight was. Didn't seem important before last night, you know what I mean?"

"Okay. So? What're we doing here, sport?" Ronnie spreads his arms out with palms up.

"Look, Ronnie, we have some time before the Atlantic City tournament. We have almost a week before the pre-tournament bullshit even starts."

"You know our strategy. We always get to wherever we're going early. Chill, kickback, no last-second rushing around."

I look at him and slowly shake my head no. "Look, Ronnie..." I think he can see how serious I am. There is no way I'm leaving here without seeing Annie some more. No way.

He gives me a grin, shrugs. "Then again, that ain't the only flight out of McCarran this week."

I give him a slap on the shoulder.

On his way to the door, he stops. "Hey, almost forgot. What about that turd she was with at the game? The one that got in your face?"

I laugh. "She's in town for the week, right? Meets him two days ago. He's a local player. She keeps seeing him around. Nice enough, she said. Showed her around the Magnum the first day she was here, they had lunch, and then yesterday they went and played some cards."

Ronnie is looking at me with a little frown.

"She told me you and I showed up and the rest is history. He's history, too. Her words, not mine. Said she couldn't believe what the crazy bastard did after the game. She wanted to crawl under a rock."

He grins now and loosens up a little.

"She never even knew the poor bastard's last name."

"Well, I don't imagine that's the first heart she's ever broken." He goes out into the hallway but then pops his head back in. "So, okay Romeo, an hour, down in the Aces 'n Eights Bar? A drink'll do you good." He gives me another wink and shuts the door behind him.

It's all in my head, but I swear I can remember her smell just then.

I remember her writing down her number, and I think it's in my sports jacket. I find the folded paper and give her a call. No answer. I decide to leave a voicemail.

"Hey, it's just me. Listen, sorry about the attempted rape last night. Seriously though, give me a call when you get a sec. I wanna make some plans, figure out what you'd like to do tomorrow. See ya."

As I hang my jacket back up from last night, I catch that whiff again. I'm glad Ronnie left, because I look like an idiot smelling my jacket.

Oh, yeah. Atlantic City can definitely wait a few days.

ELEVEN
Casey

"You've got to be kidding me!" Goatee said.

I didn't reply. Just raked in the large pot. It was over eight hundred, and a good share of it was his.

Was.

"How does a guy get trips three hands in a row?" Goatee asked, his voice louder than it needed to be.

"Trips run in threes, I guess," I said, stacking my chips and shrugging. I was riding the wave, and I didn't care what this muscle-bound amateur thought of me.

He stared at me with what was probably supposed to be an intimidating steroids glare. I gave him the flat look back. I was really tired of taking people's shit.

"That's really cute," he said, his voice low and coarse. "Maybe we could step outside, talk about numbers out there."

I shook my head. "The game's in here."

"Well, I say if you're coming on," he leaned forward intensely, "then come on."

"Easy, now," Wade said. As dealers in this town go, he was easygoing and reluctant to call security over. "This is a friendly game, y'all."

I glanced over at Wade. His nametag had his hometown under his name. San Angelo, Texas. Great. More southern charm.

"Nothing friendly about a cheat," Goatee said.

I almost groaned. You don't say "cheat" in a casino. It's like bombs and airplanes. It's never funny, and it always brings a serious response.

Wade spread the cards out, showed his sleeves, and waited. Several of the players looked confused. Goatee stared daggers at me. I ignored him, gave my chips a quick count, sat back, and waited.

Within a minute, three men in suits appeared at the table, as well as the pit boss. He was an old veteran of the strip who looked like he ought to be managing second-rate prize fighters or something.

"This table is closed," he said gruffly, "due to an allegation of misplay."

"What?" one of the other players, who I nicknamed Poindexter, asked.

"Leave your chips on the table," continued the pit boss. "Provide my proctors with your identification."

"What the hell?" asked Goatee, still clueless.

The pit boss turned to him. "We will be reviewing all hands played since you sat down at this table." He didn't bother calling Goatee "sir."

"I've been here two *hours*."

"I know. And we have to review every hand. That's what happens when a player alleges misconduct at the table." He didn't add the word "asshole," but I think everyone at the table heard it just the same.

"You're kidding."

"No, I am definitely not kidding." The pit boss looked around the table. "All of you may wait at the table while the review is taking place, or you can return when it is finished."

I laid my ID on top of my chips. "I'm going to use the bathroom and make a phone call," I told the pit boss. "And I don't want him following me."

The boss nodded. One of the suits stood between Goatee and me. I stood and walked away toward the restrooms.

I'd ridden the wave again, turning my forty into almost forty-five in just five hours. It was slow going because the stakes were small. But I was fleecing the tourists and the amateurs, so it was also easy going. I was playing it safe instead of going to the big stake tables where I might run up against some real players.

I thought about Annie, who was practicing at the minimum bet tables at the Riviera. That was who I was thinking about when I mentioned the phone call. I knew this review would take a while. I only had about five K on the table, so I could go elsewhere and start in on another game. But if I got deep into that game, I wouldn't want to break away to come back and pick up my winnings here. Better to call her up and see if she wanted to meet me in her room at the Riviera. That was a much better way to pass a couple of hours. Lose myself in her. Maybe even order some sandwiches and a beer afterward.

I strolled into the restroom and stood at the urinal. Before I could even start pissing, a piece of hard metal jammed against my back.

"Put your dick away, you fucking degenerate."

I froze. There was no mistaking the coldness in that voice. Mats.

The image of Grady's black and white checkered shoes glinting in the desert sun flashed through my brain.

Mats nudged me with the gun. "Now."

I zipped up and turned around. He turned with me. "Out, and to the right."

I walked out of the bathroom and turned right. I guessed that he had the gun inside his jacket pocket. Someone had to notice how close we close we were walking. It wasn't natural.

"That exit there, up ahead," he said.

We walked out, slick as you please, and not a single security person had a word to say about it. How fucked up is that? Some hick iron-pumper says the word "cheat" and Seal Team Six responds to the table, but Mats the Rat can stick a gun in my side and march me out the door without causing a ripple.

We got into the back seat of a white Yukon with shaded windows. Mats took the small gun out of his pocket and showed it to me. "Just so you know I'm not bluffing," he said.

I thought about telling him I didn't think he was a bluffer, just a thief, but I knew this shit had turned serious, and every smart remark would have a heavy price.

So I shut my mouth.

Mats noticed and smiled.

I looked out of the window on my side and waited. If we drove out of the city and into the desert, I was going to have to make a move on Mats. The driver couldn't do shit, and the goon in the front passenger seat wouldn't be too effective either. If I could make short work of Mats, and take his gun, I could get control of both of them in the front seat.

Easier said than done, as Mats stared at me and kept the little gun pointed at me, but in tight to his body.

I waited.

We didn't leave the city. Instead, we pulled into an industrial park, which was almost as bad. They could kill me here and just dump me in the desert later. Small razors of cold fear slashed in my lower belly.

This was bad.

"Nervous?" Mats asked, letting the "s" sound trail off in a long hiss. "I would be."

I didn't say anything. There was nothing I could say.

We pulled up to a garage door. The driver hit a button, and the door rolled up. We pulled inside the delivery bay.

All around us were pallets, stacked high with boxes of merchandise wrapped in plastic. I stared at them. Game consoles. The newest edition.

It was hard to know if this was one of the Swede's legitimate businesses or if all of this stuff was hijacked. If this was a legit business, maybe he wasn't going to whack me. Maybe this was something else. A serious talk or something. But if these consoles were swag…

"Wait," Mats said. The driver and the passenger got out of the car and positioned themselves. Then Mats waved at me with the little gun. "Out."

I wanted to feed that fucking gun to him so bad I could taste it. But this wasn't the time or the place. Even if I wasn't going to get another chance, this wasn't it.

I got out of the car and followed the two goons up a ramp and down a short hallway. The entire warehouse was dimly lit and quiet, even though it was the middle of the day. Then I realized it must be a Saturday or a Sunday. In my world, there is no weekend, but outside of the strip, most of the people still lived a nine-to-five, Monday through Friday existence.

We stepped into the bright lights of the break room. The hum of soda machines and the buzz of fluorescent lights were the only sound other than our footsteps.

At the table sat the Swede. Next to him was Babe Parcella.

Fuck.

The Swede smiled, almost as if he'd heard my thought. He sat erect, tall and thin, with a round head, thinning hair, and round eyeglasses. He looked more like an accountant than a loan shark, but I guess when you get right down to it, there isn't much of a difference.

"Mr. Brunnell," he said. "Thank you for coming."

A dozen replies shot through my head, but I knew nothing good would come from any of them. If there's one thing catching ball for so many years taught me, it was patience. And how to wait and respond to what the pitcher decides to do. How he threw the ball was outside of my control. I could only control my reaction. How I caught.

"Please, sit down," the Swede said.

Mats nudged me forward. I pulled out one of the plastic chairs and sat across from him and Babe.

"We have a few pieces of business to conduct," the Swede continued, "but we'll be quick about it, because we're all busy men, no?" He motioned toward Babe. The big man leaned forward. I had an image of the real Babe giving me some encouragement on making it to the Show, or a tip on hitting the long ball. It's crazy what your mind will do in these situations.

"The thing is, Case," Babe said, "you ain't such a good credit risk anymore. So that money I staked you? I sold the loan to Mr. Stahlberg here." He motioned toward the Swede. "All twenty-five gees," he finished.

I smiled in spite of it all. The son of a bitch had staked me ten. The Swede took debts at fifty cents on the dollar. So, by telling the Swede it was actually twenty-five, Babe Parcella, slick piece of shit that he was, would walk away with twelve five. Twenty-five hundred richer. No loss. And it was such chump change to the Swede that he didn't even care if he was getting played. He'd only add it on to my total, anyway.

"This is fucked up," I muttered, shaking my head.

It was the Swede who replied. "Not paying one's debts is, as you say, very *fucked up*." The profanity sounded strange coming from him, as if the words were not ones he usually spoke. I'd only ever had a few conversations with the man, but he seemed prissy enough to me that he probably didn't curse.

I didn't bother arguing the dollar amounts. It wouldn't do any good.

"Mr. Parcella," the Swede said, "it's been a pleasure doing business with you."

Babe rose, shook hands with the Swede, tipped me a wink, and walked out of the room.

I fucking hate people who wink.

Once Babe was gone, the Swede turned his attention to me. "Mr. Brunnell," he said, "I am saddened that we are in this situation. We go a fair distance back, you and I."

I took a deep breath and let it out, trying to relieve the tension in my body. He wouldn't buy my debt from Babe if he was planning on killing me. That's what I kept telling myself.

"All the way back to rookie ball," I agreed.

The Swede nodded. "In Clearwater. I have to say, I don't miss Florida. The heat here is worse, but it is, as they say, a *dry* heat."

"Nothing like Uppsala," I said.

That brought a smile to his face. "What is? But I fear I could no longer take the winters there. I've been too long here in the desert."

"Just like I can't catch anymore," I said, my smile turning dark. If he was going to kill me, I decided I wasn't going to lay down easy. I wouldn't push him over the edge if he hadn't made up his mind, but if this was it, I was playing hard to the final pitch. "Not after Reading, at least."

The Swede didn't look upset at all. If anything, he looked a little melancholy. "Ah, well, Mr. Brunnell, what is it that they say? We all live and learn, yes? And we both learned something about each other back then, did we not?"

"We did."

He learned that I wouldn't betray my teammates over a gambling debt. I learned that the price for not betraying my teammates to eradicate a gambling debt was high.

"And yet, we have continued our relationship here, years later. With no hard feelings. And both wiser for it."

"We have."

"And it has been a profitable relationship, has it not?"

For one of us, I thought, but I nodded.

"The problem is that you have continued to run up a large debt over the past several months. And you just become my highest debtor, Mr. Brunnell. Do you know what you owe me now?"

"One eighty," I said immediately.

He shook his head and corrected me. "Two oh five."

Shit. Babe's stake loan. That ten thousand cost me twenty-five.

"I'm working hard," I said.

"At the small tables, I'm told."

"The tourists are easy pickings. It might take me a while, but I'll build it up."

He shrugged. "Personally, I don't care how you make your

money. All I care is that you pay me mine."

"I'm working on it," I repeated.

"That's commendable. You have three days."

"*Three?*"

"That is correct. The full amount will be due, along with interest, at the end of the third day. Let's round it up to...shall we say two twenty-five? That seems like a fair figure. Low interest, as these things go."

So much for playing the small tables. I'd have to go up against the whales and the pros to get up to two and a quarter in just three days. Which raised the risk that I'd take a bad beat at any point along the way.

Of course, that's if the Swede was being straight with me. He could just be planting false hope with this three-day shit. This could be the end of the road and he just wanted me to be relaxed about it, unsuspecting. It'd go easy that way.

"I believe that's all I wished to communicate to you, Mr. Brunnell." The Swede stood. "Mats still has a matter to discuss, however."

The Swede walked toward the door.

"Hey," I called out.

He stopped. He cocked his head to listen to me.

"Call me Casey," I said.

"Pardon?"

"For the whole time we've known each other, you've called me by my last name. If you're planning to kill me, at least call me Casey."

He didn't move for a moment. Then he said, "Good day, Mr. Brunnell," and left the room.

I didn't even have time to breathe a sigh of relief before Mats and his goons were on me. One of them grabbed my right arm and held it tight. The other snaked his arm around my neck and clamped down. I reached up with my free left hand, but Mats snatched it at the wrist and slammed it onto the table.

Dark walls clawed at the edge of my vision, starting to close in as the thug squeezed. Just as the two walls were about to slam together, he loosened slightly. His grip was still strong, though, and I couldn't move.

Mats appeared in front of my face. He gave me a cruel smile. "You know what I heard, Casey?" he said. "I heard there's not much of a future playing five card draw these days. That no one hardly plays it anymore. You hear that?"

I struggled in the grasp of the man behind me, but he was just too strong.

"So you do get me, then? *Du förstå?*" He smiled. "Maybe we should find you some checkered shoes, my friend. Because we both know you are eventually going to the same place Grady did."

I tried to tell him to go fuck himself but could only manage a gurgle. My temples throbbed.

"Don't try so hard," Mats said. "It only makes things worse."

He squeezed my left wrist. His grip was vise-like, almost seeming to paralyze my hand.

"That's a good *pojke*." He pulled something from his pocket and made a flicking motion. The sound of steel snapping into place echoed through the room.

"Nothing is free," Mats said. "Especially not loan extensions."

Too late, I saw. It didn't matter, though. I couldn't break free of the man behind me or the one who gripped my right arm. Mats had an iron grip on my left wrist, and I could barely feel my fingers. I was powerless, and the more I struggled, the closer I came to being choked unconscious.

"At least you're an honest player," Mats said, "and not a mechanic. Otherwise, this could be a real career ender for you." He paused. "Then again, being an honest player might be why you're where you're at right now."

He shrugged, then lowered the knife to where he had my hand pressed out on the break room table. Without a word, he levered the sharp blade down in one swift motion, taking off the last joint of my pinky finger.

Frank Zafiro and Jim Wilsky

I tried to scream but blacked out instead.

TWELVE
Cord

It's about seven or so now and the huge Aces 'n Eights Bar is filling up with the usual Vegas mix. We have a good back-corner table in the large elevated section.

There are people you definitely recognize from entertainment, sports, and the business world. Trump had been here last year, and he didn't disappoint. He was the ass I had fully expected and then some.

Then comes the next level. People you see around all the time, no matter which big casino you're at. People with money to spend, win or lose. They want to be there, be seen. Wouldn't miss it for the world. Some are friends of mine, and others in this group look familiar, but I can't quite put a name to the face.

Then, finally, there are the wannabes. Dressed okay, actually way better than okay, really. Roll of money in the pocket but not in the bank. They always talk a little too loud and laugh a little too hard. I've played them in tournaments before, and they win some money, but they never win big. Never will, and always praying for that river card to bail them out. It never does, when it really matters.

Ronnie breaks up my thoughts by standing up, and the others at the table do too. My mind always wanders when I'm bored, and I love to people watch anyway. I've been nodding but not even listening to what these guys have just been talking about.

"Okay, well, this is good." Ronnie claps his hands softly. "Gentlemen, we shall see you in AC in just a few days, then. We'll also have an answer back to you quickly on the commercial appearance with the other three top players you choose."

"Cord, always good...a pleasure. Ronnie, thanks again." Marv Plochman nods, smiles stiffly, and sticks his hand out like a robot. "Good luck in Atlantic City."

Marvin had been a good player once, but that skill doesn't necessarily transfer over to being a good President of the World Poker Association.

As soon as we get done shaking hands and slapping backs with ol' Marvin and his new idiot CFO, we sit down and Ronnie snags a passing waitress. He holds up two fingers.

"Something I need to talk to you about, pardner," he says to me.

"Uh, no. No, you can't watch Annie and me from the other room tomorrow night."

"Serious now. This is serious." Ronnie's eyes are always scanning, and as soon as he says that, he stands up again. "Right after we're through here."

Making their way through the crowd comes a small entourage. The Magnum people had been hovering nearby for the chance to get the formalities over with. Three of them come weaving their way over. Michael Carlese, the hotel owner, along with some ass from the Nevada gaming commission that I'd met before, but I can't remember his name for the life of me...and the big guy from last night. Tony or Tommy? No wait...it was Babe. Yeah, Babe.

After hellos, we all stand with our hands in our pockets and chat for a minute. The girl comes back around with our drinks, and Ronnie waves his hand around our group, gives her three fingers, then says something in her ear. She nods and leaves.

Ronnie turns to the group. "What can I get you guys? Least I can do is buy you your own beer, in your own bar." He laughs and smiles that million-dollar smile.

"No, Ronnie, we really have to go. Just wanted to say thank

you for playing this year and bringing the star power here, in the person of Cord."

It's my turn, I guess.

"Mr. Carlese, pleasure was all mine. The Magnum is the best there is." I smile just like Ronnie did. "Anywhere. I tell everyone that."

"Excellent. Excellent. Thank you."

Handshakes all around. Shits and grins everywhere. They start to head off.

"Oh, two things before you go." I just don't know when to shut the hell up sometimes.

"Sure, Cord. What is it?" Carlese smiles, turns back to me.

"First is a request. Actually, it's a must." I look at Ronnie and then back at Carlese, my face is just serious as hell. Ronnie has got that *oh shit* look in his eyes. I give it a little pause.

"Don't invite the damn Frenchman next year. I mean it. If that little frog is here, I ain't."

The three Magnum guys look at each other.

I don't say anything more. It's a long five seconds.

"Well, Cord...I..."

I put my hand on Carlese's shoulder softly and smile. Then I give them a laugh.

Another pause and then Ronnie kicks in with a chuckle. Laughs all around now.

"Shit, Cord, you had me going there." Carlese shook his head and wagged his finger at me. "I'm almost scared to ask about the second thing."

I take a sip of my Maker's and smile.

"Second thing, and I *am* serious on this one. Babe here needs to be promoted or get a raise or some damn thing. He bent over backwards for us during our stay."

I look at Babe and smile. He shakes his head no, all humble and shit. Smiles back at me. There is something in that smile, though. Definitely something in his eyes.

"You know, you're right. I pay him a boatload as it is, but it is salary review time." Carlese slaps Babe on his broad back. "No wonder you wanted to come with us to say goodbye to Cord." He laughs again.

Babe leans into our huddle a little more. "Very kind of you, Mr. Needham. Just doing my job. It was great having you here. Thanks for coming this year." His eyes are still saying something. He gives Ronnie a sideways glance. Cordial. At best.

"Thanks to you, too, Mr. Turnbull."

After they left, we both sit back down, and I pull the first passing waitress over again.

"Two more, buttercup," I say. And just so we're clear here, she is most definitely a buttercup. "Two more Maker's and a splash of water."

"You betcha, Mr. Needham."

"If you call me mister again, I think I'll just curl up and die."

She smiles and melts into the crowd but not before giving me a little look back over her shoulder.

The rest of the night was totally open, but no Annie. That would have to wait until tomorrow. Then again, no more bullshit like we've been doing for the last two hours.

"Ronnie, I know I've said it a million times, but I *really* hate that part of this business." I tip my almost empty glass in the direction of where the Magnum boys had been standing.

He doesn't say anything. Just looks at me. He can get that way sometimes, so I just let it go and watch the crowd.

Then he pulls out his cell phone and scrolls down and around on his screen. That reminds me of Annie, and I pull mine out too. No voicemail from her, but it was still early, basically the equivalent of frickin' noon here in Vegas.

Ronnie puts the cell phone down on the table and says, "Where'd she have to go for those fucking drinks, the twentieth floor?"

"She just now left, man. What the hell is the problem here? You're acting like an ass, and that's my job."

"You don't want to know what the problem is, Cord. You

really don't."

"Is this what you were talking about being serious about, right before the Magnum group came by?"

"Yup."

"Well, come on, spill it. You wanted to tell me earlier and now you don't think so?"

He's staring straight ahead. "I need that drink she's having shipped in from the East Coast first."

And just like that she expertly slips in between and around two guys with the drink tray, heading our way.

"Well, there she is. I'm glad you're back, because Ronnie here—"

"Thanks," Ronnie says, cutting me off. She puts the glasses in front of us. "Probably need two more pretty quick. We're on a mission." He gives her a stiff smile.

I look at the name tag. "Lindsey, don't be a stranger now, and..."

"Okay, okay, thanks." Ronnie takes a little sip of the drink, then looks at her and sets the glass down firmly. "Thanks again."

"Sure, sure, I'll be back shortly." She smiles a little awkwardly, looks at him, and then at me. Off she goes.

"Man, you are a *smooth* one with the ladies. I'm, like, very jealous over here."

"I thought you were all in love, Casanova?"

"Doesn't mean I can't flirt it up a little."

"Anyway."

"Anyway what, asshole? What's this *serious* problem that you want to talk about, but you won't tell me what it is?"

He half turns in his chair and leans into my direction. His chin is out and up a little. Mouth just a straight tight line. Still doesn't say anything.

"Okay, Ronnie, cut the shit. Tell me what we have going on here."

He leans in a little closer and lets out a sigh.

"The Aruba Royale."

The bar is getting noisy, but I hear him. The look on his face is getting worse. A hundred things about that night are going through my head, and they're all bad.

"Okay. Yeah. What about it? I mean, what, man? *What the fuck about it?*" I'm talking quiet, trying to stay calm and focused about this, but it ain't working. "Talk to me. Now."

Ronnie looks at me, his expression tight. He takes another drink and shakes his head back and forth slowly. "After I left your room, I called downstairs and told them we'd be staying a day or two more. So, we're all set there."

"Well, damn, that's good, huh? Somehow, I don't think that's what we're talking about here though…right? C'mon, Ronnie, we been together too long. Stop dancing and just tell me."

"Twenty minutes later, I'm waiting for you to meet me down here, I'm sitting right here, and I get a call." He takes a little too big of a drink, winces a little, and then runs a shaky hand through his hair.

I decide to ease up and wait, give him some time. This shit is not good, whatever it is.

"It's Babe Parcella," he continues. "He says, hey, that's great about us staying around for a few more days. Then he says, it's funny timing because he needs to talk to me about a phone call he got this morning. Then I ask Parcella if there was some kind of a problem, you know?"

I'm the one who takes the big drink this time, and I see our little Lindsey out of the corner of my eye. I hold up a hand with two fingers and she sees, nodding her head. She turns on the bright smile at first, but it fades quickly. The look on my face must be bad, and she just gives me another quick nod.

"He says to me that in his line of work, he has run into all sorts: good, bad, and shaky. Well, he just keeps going. He says an old acquaintance of his had called him. A guy he had to fire two years ago. The call was about us, Cord. About Aruba."

He takes another big drink and pulls out a new pack of Marlboro Lights. Ronnie hasn't smoked for three years.

"So, what else did he say?" I ask. "Who is this guy that called Babe?"

"All he said is that the guy is dangerous. Didn't name him. Parcella said the guy knows all about four years ago, or at least is claiming to. Threatened to do some things, say some things. Babe was very vague, though, and said he didn't want talk details on the phone."

"So, he's gonna help us with this guy?"

"That's what he says. Wants us to meet him offsite tomorrow. Around three in the afternoon or so. He'll let me know where."

"All right, so we don't really know if this mystery guy has anything or not. I mean, it ain't a total secret, Ronnie. This guy could just be bluffing. Going off an old article or something."

"Don't think so, pardner. I think he knows."

"Why? I mean, sure, it got out a little, but we held it together good. Ironclad fucking alibi. You nailed it down there, man. You saved our asses."

Ronnie stares off and frowns.

"What, man?"

He turns and looks at me.

"Parcella is gonna play this." His eyes are boring into me. "He knows what really happened somehow. I can tell."

I look at him while knocking down the rest of my drink. Fuck me.

"He's not only gonna play this. He's gonna play *us,* Cord." He finishes his drink, too.

"But fuck, why?"

"Because he can."

THIRTEEN
Casey

When I woke up in the desert, I thought for a few moments that I was dead. That, somehow, this was the afterlife. No heaven, no hell. Just wandering around the world, revisiting all the failures in it.

The pulse of pain in my left hand convinced me I wasn't dead. Or, if I was, then it was hell and not heaven. Which made perfect fucking sense.

I shook my head and sat up slowly. That's when I realized I wasn't even out in the desert. I was in a sandy, empty lot behind a grocery store, not a mile away from the industrial warehouse where I met the Swede.

Shit. I shopped here sometimes.

Another sharp throb from my hand. I lifted it to look at it. A wad of brown paper towels was wrapped around my ring and small fingers. I remembered the knife levering down, taking a joint from my small finger. Did he take the ring finger, too? After I passed out?

I snatched at the paper towel, but as soon as I brushed up against it, a shock wave blasted up my hand and arm. I let out a sharp cry of pain and surprise. Then, gingerly, I picked at the makeshift dressing, unraveling it a bit at a time. When I pulled the last piece off, I stared at the swollen pinkie. It was an angry, raw red, punctuated with crimson burn marks and traces of burned black marks.

My ring finger was untouched.

I should've figured. Mats wouldn't want to waste all that good torture on an unconscious man who couldn't feel it. And the cauterization made it less likely that I'd go to the hospital, too. He was a thinking man's thug.

I let out a deep, jagged sigh. When I rolled to my knees and pushed myself to my feet, I winced in pain. Moving hurt. Hell, breathing hurt.

I walked carefully toward the grocery store. The uneven ground made every step seem jarring, and every motion felt like a hammer pounding on my hand. I gritted my teeth and kept on, grateful when I reached pavement.

I paused for a moment and took inventory with my right hand. Keys were in the right front. Where was my car? After a moment, I realized it was still parked at the casino. Shit. Along with my ID and my pile of chips. Oh well. At least they'd hold it for me at the cashier's.

I patted my back pocket. My wallet was still there. I took it out and looked inside. All the cash was gone. Fucking Mats. I fumbled with it and found my cards were all still inside, including my debit card. How much money did I have in my bank account? I figured a few hundred bucks or so. Enough to get home, clean up, get to the casino, and get my money there. And get back to work, fucked up hand or not. I put the wallet back in my pocket and continued on my way.

When I made it around the side of the store and through the front doors, the rush of cool air that met me felt wonderful. I made my way to the first aid section, found some gauze, some medical tape, and antibacterial ointment. I knew burns were prone to infection, and nasty ones, too. I don't know where I heard that, but it was probably on a Discovery channel documentary or something. Education by cable television is underrated.

I threw some maximum strength pain reliever in the basket, too.

I should go to the ER, I knew. But as much as I hated to admit it, Mats was right to think I wouldn't. There would be too many questions. And they'd probably call the cops. And the cops would definitely call Nicky.

Besides, what would they do? Rinse it off with some saline, apply some antibacterial ointment, wrap it in gauze, and prescribe me some painkillers, that's what. I had all of that already in my little red basket.

When I got to the checkout stand, the guy at the register saw my finger. He shot me a concerned look, but I put my hand behind my back and gave him a weak smile. After a moment, he shrugged and rang up my items. I figured he'd seen worse, and what happens in Vegas...

After I paid and got some cash back, I asked the checker to call for a cab. One rolled up outside twenty minutes later. I gave the driver my address and sat back in the seat, my plastic bag on my lap. Every start and stop with this guy was a jerk and a jolt. I gritted my teeth and tried to endure it, but after six blocks, I couldn't take it anymore.

"Easy!" I snapped at him. "I'm nursing the hangover from hell back here."

He scowled but didn't say anything. After that, he drove with exaggerated care, taking his time, running up the fare. I didn't care.

At my apartment, I paid him and waited for my change. When he handed it back to me, I turned to go.

"What?" He yelled after me "No tip?"

I turned and stared at him, blinking. Did he know what just happened to my finger? "Is that some kind of sick joke?" I asked.

He gave me a confused look. "No." Then he shook his head and waved at me dismissively. "Fucking cheapskate. Go ahead. Lose it at the crap tables." He dropped the cab into gear and pulled away.

I stood, watching him go. Then I realized how completely paranoid I had to be to ask a question like that.

My next thought was that paranoid was better than dead.

At my apartment door, I put the shopping bag on the ground instead of trying to hold it in my left hand while I used the key. The air inside was stuffy and hot. I turned on the air conditioner. It made a grinding, labored noise and started up. Whether there'd be anything more than a trickle of cool air was anyone's guess.

I threw some ice cubes in a bowl and added water from the tap. I sat at the kitchen table, spreading my doctoring supplies out in front of me. Gently, I lowered the maimed finger into the ice water.

It hurt at first. A lot. But it was more like a sharp knife than a pounding sledge. Slowly, the pain dulled. After a while, I wished I'd thought to grab a beer from the fridge before I sat down. Then I remembered I'd finished off the last of them yesterday. I'd need to go out if I was going to get a drink.

And I needed a drink.

After what seemed like forever, I removed the finger from the ice water and dabbed it dry with a piece of gauze. Then I used another piece to slather on the antibacterial cream. Finally, I wrapped it carefully in a loose dressing. I secured it with tape, looping it around the base of my finger, over the back of my hand and across the palm a couple of times.

"There you go," I whispered to no one. "Just saved yourself seven hundred bucks."

I popped four pain relievers in my mouth and drank from the faucet to wash them down. Then I turned and leaned against the counter by the sink.

Now what?

As if in answer, the phone rang. I started a little, then cursed. That fucking Mats had me jumping at shadows.

I picked up the phone but didn't push the talk button. The caller ID read "Raines, Nicollete." I sighed and shook my head. I wasn't ready to talk to her.

After the fourth ring, my answering machine kicked in. I waited, and in a few moments, Nicky's voice came over the speaker. "Casey? You there?"

She sounded worried to me, but maybe I was projecting.

"If you're there, pick up."

I had no intention of doing that.

"Casey? I've got a bad feeling about something. I don't know what, but I want...I *need* to talk to you."

Shit. Her bad feelings were as dangerous as her hunches. She wouldn't quit until she figured out why she was feeling that way. I could put off calling her for a day, maybe two, but no more...

"I wish you had a cell phone like everyone else," she said. "Call me as soon as you get this."

"No," I said, but my voice came out in a croaked whisper. I had no idea what I was going to say to her, so it was better just to avoid the conversation until I had everything straightened out.

"Casey, are you there?" Now her voice was suspicious. "If you are, you better pick up the goddamn phone."

Shit. The woman wasn't psychic, but...*shit*. She was damn intuitive. Or I was too predictable.

The line stayed open for a few more seconds, then she hung up.

I sighed. She was coming over. I knew it. And I couldn't deal with her yet. Not the questions, the interrogation, and what if she started in about Babe Parcella?

I pulled Annie's white card out of my wallet and punched in her number. She answered on the third ring. I could hear the sounds of the casino floor in the background. "Hey, you," she said, almost in a purr. "I was just thinking about you."

"Yeah?" I asked. I wasn't entirely immune to her flirting, even over the phone, but I was in enough pain to say back, "Your thoughts involve a guy getting the shit kicked out of him?"

"What's wrong?" she asked, her voice immediately full of concern. "What happened?"

"I got in a jam," I said. "And I got fucked up."

She was quiet for a minute. Then she asked, "What can I do?"

"I could use some doctoring," I said, staring down at my bandaged hand. "And...a friend."

"Let me cash out my chips. Where are you?"

"I'll meet you at your room," I said.

She hung up without a word. So did I. Then I walked my ass out of that stuffy, hot apartment and hoofed it several blocks to a convenience store, where I used the payphone to call another cab. The one that pulled up was being driven by a woman with a long braid. Beads hung from the rearview mirror and light bamboo flute music filled inside of the taxi.

I got in. "The Riviera," I told her.

She smiled. "You got it, my friend," she said.

I told myself maybe my luck was changing.

"Oh, my God!" Annie said, putting her hand to her mouth. "What happened?"

I stood in the hotel hallway. I must have looked like hell. Sweaty, dirty, smelly, and a bandaged-up hand. So, her reaction shouldn't have been a surprise. But it was. Somehow, I expected her to be cool and collected. Not distraught.

"Can I come in?"

"Of course!" She swung open the door. I walked in. "You're limping," she said.

"I am?"

She nodded, her eyes full of concern. "Tell me what happened."

I pointed at the door. "You want to close that?"

She glanced at the door, then let go of the handle, and turned back to me. "Tell me." The door slammed shut, but she didn't notice. All of her attention was on me, and her focus was intense. "Is it broken? How did it happen?"

I let out a strangled little laugh. I meant it to be ironic, but it only sounded weak and defeated. I sank into the chair nearest the door. "It's...gone," I said.

"Gone?" Her brow furrowed. "What...what's that mean?"

I held up my hand. "They cut it off, Annie." Tears rushed up in my throat, and I tried to swallow. It didn't matter. I felt them splash down my cheeks. "I owe money," I croaked. "I owe money, and the fuckers took my finger, and if I don't pay them, I'm going to end up in a shallow grave out in the fucking desert."

Her expression was stricken at first, but then she gave way to tears as well. She knelt next to me and pulled me forward into her embrace. The scent of her hair was the cleanest, most beautiful smell I could ever remember.

"They won't," she whispered. "They won't."

"Jesus," I whispered back. "I'm sorry."

"Don't be sorry. It's not your fault." She stroked the nape of my neck with her fingertips and brushed her lips across my cheek.

"I'm not weak," I told her.

"I know." Her voice was so soothing.

"I'm not," I said, but with less force.

She didn't answer, just stroked my neck. I drank in her presence, her comfort. This wasn't like Nicky. There were no demands here, no rigid needs. No expectations, no judgment. Just softness and strength, and maybe something more, too. Something deeper.

"They're not going to hurt you anymore, baby," she whispered, her voice quiet but sure. "We won't let them."

FOURTEEN
Cord

Ronnie, or his girl, have turned the damn music off again. When did that happen, a minute ago or an hour ago?

"Ronnie...? Hey, Ronnie?"

It was darker than dark down here. The hotel was up a rise and to the left, behind us. I turned slowly and looked back at it, then I let myself fall back onto the warm sand. One arm was under her slim waist and my other was stretched way out, gripping a bottle of whiskey...or maybe rum. I was drunk, so was she, and man, it just didn't get any better than this.

The soft surf that breaks created a little light in the inky darkness, but not much. Plenty of twinkling stars up there, but no moon tonight. There was a fishing boat way the hell out there. Its lights were moving very slowly, left to right. I think it was moving, or maybe it was just me.

Vera was lying next to me, very close, a shadow on the lighter sand. Her body was sleek and very dark, both her smooth, brown skin and coal black hair. She smiled at me when I looked down at her and rolled to her side and up on an elbow. She ain't got a stitch a clothes on and neither did I.

"Ahhhh, *mi amante. Amannnnte.*" She grinned lazily, and the white of her eyes were slowly shuttered as she either fell asleep or passed out, or both. Her head slipped slowly off her hand and went to the sand.

When her head and shoulder lowered, two figures came into view in the distance, walking up the beach towards us. As they came, I could barely see the soft surf foam that gathered around their ankles briefly before receding again.

There was a gentle warm breeze tonight, and I could feel it ruffle my hair. Despite the heat, the breeze gave me a quick chill. Maybe it was the two approaching figures. Something wasn't right.

"Ronnie? Hey, heads up." I thought he was over with what's-her-name, behind a small dune about thirty yards away.

I looked down at Vera, who was smiling in her sleep. Raising my eyes to the two figures walking up the beach, I realized they were trotting now. Trotting fast, leaving the water's edge and coming straight for Vera and me.

"Ronnie?" I said it louder this time.

Nothing but the soft surf sound.

I stood up and took one step forward and two back.

I heard one of the two approaching yell something, almost a scream. Vera sat up straight, like a shot, and started grabbing around for her clothes.

"No, Ernesto. NO!"

The two guys, one big, one much smaller, were about fifty feet away now. The trot slowed, and they walked again. They kind of separated, too, like they wanted to flank me. The smaller one had a white tunic on, almost like a uniform. Wait. I remembered then, it was what like the staff wore at the hotel.

"Ohhhh, *tu eres una puta*!" the big one growled.

"No, no, no..." Vera looked at me and then back at the big one. Ernesto, I guess. She ran to him wailing, with arms reaching out. He slapped her, then roundhouse punched her, hard to the sand. She curled up as I came towards the big dude. Guy was over six foot and built like a tank. Tattoos everywhere.

He loomed over her. She was crying and sobbing. As I got near them, he reached into a pocket of the baggy shorts he's wearing. The night and surf were so quiet, and maybe my mind just made it up, but I saw that long, pencil-thin switchblade pop out before I heard the click. And I know I heard that click, because I can still hear it sometimes.

Then the other girl yipped three times, short little cries, then screamed long and hard from somewhere off to my right.

I was spooked now. I didn't want to fight. Truth was, I never really looked for it, but I will. Hell, I had to fight, or I just run off. And that ain't gonna happen.

I had maybe fifteen feet in between him and me. I was spooked because hey, I've been in plenty of scraps and all, but I never been in a damn knife fight. Especially one where the other guy has the only knife.

"Hey, you son of a *bitch*."

He just kept looking down at her.

"I said, HEY, YOU! FUCKHEAD!"

Ten feet now, but there was a new problem. Out of the corner of my eye, the little guy in the white uniform was coming in from my right side. A little ways off but coming all the same.

I threw him a quick glance and realized with big eyes that he had a knife too, a much bigger one. It's like a carving knife in a kitchen or something. Little fucker must be a cook at the hotel.

Then I saw Ronnie. Dripping wet from the ocean. Nice time for a swim, Ronnie. He had his finger up to his mouth because he saw me notice him. The little guy had his back to Ronnie as he came trotting in from the shore.

I remembered Vera crying, pleading for forgiveness. She rolled over to look up at him with her hands reaching up. She saw the knife though, and screamed. He knelt, knife held high and away from her arms. He was in a rage and possessed with doing her, because he never looked up at me. He just never saw me coming, or maybe he did and didn't care.

I hit him high and hard, like a linebacker trying to take a head off. He was just getting ready to cut her or stab her. I was almost too late, because a drunk running in sand ain't the quickest thing you ever saw. But I nailed him and nailed him good.

On top of the body shot I gave him, we hit our heads together hard and he definitely got the worst of that. I remember it hurting like hell and getting the stars a little, but he looked and acted way worse off.

When I rolled away and stood up, he tried to do the same, but his legs were wobbly, and his head wasn't right. He staggered sideways and went to a knee, then put an arm down to the sand for more support. I looked over at Vera, and she had stopped crying finally.

Turns out I was a little late after all. The long, thin blade was sticking up almost perfectly vertical to her chest. Buried to the hilt. I saw her leg move a little, more of a twitch probably.

That's when I heard Ronnie and the other guy. There was a lot of grunting and growling going on behind me. A yell in Spanish. Ronnie shouted something my brain couldn't register, but I know it was his voice.

I met the dazed and confused eyes of the big boy, and I guess I just went *loco*, as they say down here. When I hit him with a shoulder again, he saw me coming, but all he did was put up a wavering hand to fend me away. I heard the air whoosh out of him when he hit the sand, and then I straddled him.

Behind me, I heard a man scream, short, high pitched, and when it slowly died out, whoever it was died out too. You could just tell by that soft gargle at the end.

If it was Ronnie that had just screamed, I was dead because I was gonna kill this big bastard. Didn't care if I got a knife in my back or not, this fucker right here was going away for good.

I beat on him until I couldn't hardly swing anymore. I was gassed. I had sobered right up, but man, I was gassed. When the adrenaline finally went away, there was nothing in the tank.

I stopped, got off him, and stood shakily, staring down at a gory monster. His face was a bloody, misshapen mess. I had rearranged things. He looked dead, but his chest was still going up and down slightly.

I remembered a man screaming before and whirled around.

Almost fell down turning that quick. Ronnie was standing there staring at me. He was holding that big-ass knife.

Behind him was the thin, white line of soft surf breaking, and then it melted away. It was dark and all, but I could still see he was covered in blood. It looked black, not red. Like tar, not blood.

Holy shit, what had happened? Man, we're some kind of fucked here.

Ronnie stepped forward now.

"Cord. Cord! Hey, we gotta go man."

"I...we, hey, what the fuck, Ronnie?" I turned a small circle with my arms out and saw Vera, who was perfectly still now, the big Ernesto just a bloody lump, and over behind where Ronnie stood, I saw the little kitchen fucker sprawled out. His white tunic was black with blood and so was the sand around him. "Ronnie, what...why did this happ—"

"Cord we gotta go. I mean it. Go. Like right NOW."

"Okay, my man. Okay, brother my. We go to got away." I'm talking no sense.

"Okay, look." He looked around the beach, the whites of his eyes were big and wide. "First, the blood."

I could hear Ronnie talking, but he was down in a tunnel or something, a long way off.

"She. Your girls, yours okay now?" Even my voice was far off. There was an echo to it.

"No."

I remember Ronnie looking around and scanning the darkness again.

"Ronnie...I...my..." My voice and thoughts were all scrambled.

"Cord, we gotta go now!" He holds my head still with his two hands and tries to look into my eyes. He frowns then. "C'mon man."

"What? What the fuck, Ronnie?"

Then he had me by the arm and we were running, half stumbling towards the ocean. His grip was sliding because there was so much blood on me, and him.

As we're running, I heard it again. The click from the big guy's switchblade. We were almost to the water, and I heard Vera scream but much louder this time. Louder still comes the little guy's death-rattling scream. I was scared now, really scared. Vera screamed again, and then we were in the water and…I couldn't breathe…couldn't…I CAN'T BREATHE…

I come up fast, and I can't catch my breath. Just can't get it. I'm raining sweat, and the sheets are all tangled up around me. The sheets feel like they're trying to hold me, and I about half lose it just trying to get unwrapped from them.

I'm actually fighting to get out. Almost some kind of weird panic attack. I come rolling out sideways onto the carpet and then stand there facing the bed like I'm gonna kick its ass. Fear makes you do really stupid shit.

I used to have these dreams about once a week. Then gradually they tapered off to where I didn't have them but one, maybe two times a year. They always come back though. Always.

The dreams are like a movie, and I'm watching myself, everyone, and everything happen on a big screen. This one, though, this one was over the top, like a fucking Broadway show or something.

I just don't let myself think about that night much anymore. I can't do it. I can't allow it.

I'm still standing here and still trying to get my damn breathing settled down. The sun is piercing through slits in the long drapes, but I have no idea what time it is. I'm sure it's late though, because Ronnie and I had our last drink on the balcony when the sky was getting light in the east.

Four fucking years ago, and it seems like yesterday that it all came down. Worst day of my life. Wrong place, wrong time and sure as hell, wrong girls.

Earlier that day, I had won my first major WPA sponsored tournament. We had proceeded to tear it up all night in the Sand Bar nightclub at the Aruba Royale. Man, we had us a time. We closed the Sand Bar.

So, we took the party out to the beach, bringing booze and ice buckets, and because both girls were hotel waitresses they had to meet us out there on the sly. We were all drunk, but not really stumblin' drunk. It was late, real late, maybe three or four in the morning.

When the two jealous boyfriends finally found their missing girlfriends, it was all over but the shoutin'. The only one of them to live was the big bastard that stabbed Vera.

The Mexican police just piled the deaths of the little hotel cook, his girlfriend, and Vera's murder on old Ernesto. Ernesto was an ex-con. On top of that, he was the last man standing that night which made him the perfect fall guy. One that the police were all too willing to point to and wrap everything up all nice and neat. Less work that way.

Ernesto, after recovering from the beating, had some minor swelling of the brain and almost a total memory loss of that night. He remembers fighting but that's it, he says. He doesn't know who or why. Everyone thinks he's lying, of course. He's screwed.

We had been questioned briefly only because we'd been seen in the bar earlier with the girls. Ronnie had taken care of the rest. He got us cleaned up, got us back to the rooms. Neither of us had bloody clothes. He got himself sobered up and had a late breakfast with his brother and sister-in-law. I've known both of them as long as I've known Ronnie.

As it turns out, as the official story goes, we had been drinking with them that night after the bar closed down. Turns out no one ever said any different and no one even blinked anyway. I don't think that any law enforcement even bothered talking to Ronnie's brother.

We had dodged a serious bullet. A real serious bullet.

Until now.

Later today, we had that meeting with Babe Parcella. The only two guys who could have any true knowledge of that night were Ernesto and Ronnie's brother. Maybe Ernesto had somehow got out of his life sentence, paroled, released from prison, maybe? Or maybe it's Ronnie's brother, but I just can't believe that. Or maybe there was another set of eyes that night?

I pick my cell phone up off the nightstand. There's a blurred five or six names and numbers as I try to focus. One of them is Annie. That makes me smile, but it goes away quick. I can't let this thing with Aruba fuck with how things go with her.

Ronnie isn't gonna like it, but I've already decided on inviting her to the Atlantic City Tournament. Even with the Aruba thing going on, I don't care. My mind is flooded with her all of a sudden, and I want her. Want her right now. I'll call her as soon as I find out from Ronnie exactly when and where the Babe meeting is.

Then that night in Aruba comes sneaking back to the edge of my thoughts.

This is bullshit. I trudge off to take a shower.

I slide the glass door closed, reach out to turn the water on, and I hear Vera scream again. A piercing scream. I close my eyes and turn the dial toward hot.

FIFTEEN
Casey

I woke up before she did. Gently, I slid out of the bed and sat naked in the chair nearby. One moment, my entire body felt alive and wired and content and thrilled all at once, the aftermath of being with Annie all night. The next moment, my hand throbbed sharply and reminded me of the real world.

I smiled ruefully. Real world or lover's world, seems as if I got fucked in both. But I much preferred Annie's way over the Swede's.

The air conditioner filled the room with a steady hum. Somewhere down the hallway, I heard a door close heavily, but other than that, the hotel was fairly quiet. Six in the morning till eleven was prime sleeping time in places like this. As the blood-red numbers on the clock marched slowly toward noon, I knew things would pick up. But for now, I sat and watched Annie sleep, listened to my body sigh and wince, and tried to think of nothing else.

It didn't work for long.

A small worm of uncertainty crept into my gut. I didn't have time to just sit here, no matter how good it felt, how beautiful she looked, or even how nice her hair and body smelled. I needed to get my money from the cashier and put it to work at the bigger tables. The Swede wasn't bluffing. He'd shown me that when he dumped Grady and his checkered shoes out in the desert.

Grady. A fucking institution in this town. Jesus, things were changing. I heard it told that once upon a time, the most you'd take for a bad debt was a worse beating. It was just good business, because then the debt was still owed, and the guy could work on repaying it. But now, when the time ran out on a guy, it ran out completely.

What was I going to do? I was good at poker, sure. Damn good. Probably better than some of those hotshots who played on TV, but I never had the connections or the pretty-boy looks to get my shot. The few times I was in a position to play my way in, the luck wave broke on the beach and left me stranded. That's not something you can predict, either. Just fucking happens.

So, just like my baseball career, it would seem I was relegated to playing in the minors. Hell, that wasn't so bad, really. A guy can make a living at that. Maybe not a killing, but a living. And the difference with poker is that you don't have to worry about your body failing you sometime in your late thirties, leaving you without options. Poker is a sport you can play until you die.

Yeah, like Grady did.

I sighed.

Annie stirred, then opened her eyes and looked up at me. She smiled, and her green eyes seemed to shine. "'Morning," she murmured sleepily.

I smiled back. "Morning back."

She patted the empty space on the bed beside her. I rose and walked to the bed. She looked down at my cock, then back to my face, a mischievous smile touching her lips.

I slid into bed beside her, and for a while, there was nothing else to say.

Afterward, I lay on my back, her head nestled on my chest.

"I can hear your heartbeat," she said quietly.

"Yeah."

"It's a strong heartbeat," she said. "You know what that

means?"

"Low cholesterol?"

"No, silly." She nudged me in the side with her knuckles. "It means you're brave."

I laughed a little. "Brave? That's a good one."

"I'm serious," she said.

"I'm not brave."

"Sure you are. Look at the situation you're in."

"That situation makes me stupid, maybe, or unlucky, but not brave."

She shook her head. Her silky hair rubbed against my chest and throat. "What's important is how you deal with a situation. And you face it. You face your problem. That's brave."

I didn't answer. If she knew what kind of fear was crawling around inside my gut, she wouldn't think I was brave.

"Actually, I think you're more than brave," she said. "You're...I don't know. Heroic, maybe."

I laughed again, but this time only a little bit. When she didn't laugh, too, my own tapered off into silence.

"You're crazy," I said. "I'm not brave, and I'm definitely not heroic."

"You are," she said, her tone certain. "You've trusted me. You're helping me, even though you've got big problems of your own."

She had me there.

I didn't answer. After a moment, she gave me a long, hard squeeze.

After a long while, hunger drove us from the bed. We ordered some room service and tag-teamed the shower. When it was my turn, I wrapped a plastic sleeve for the ice bucket around my injured hand. Then I held it out of the way of the shower spray while I scrubbed my body clean with my other hand.

When I came out of the bathroom, breakfast had arrived. We

tore into it, devouring eggs, bacon, and French toast and sucking down coffee from oversized mugs.

"What's your plan?" she asked me in between bites.

"For?"

"Getting out of the situation you're in."

I shoveled some scrambled eggs into my mouth and thought about it while I chewed. After I swallowed, I said, "I have to win. That's all there is to it. Win big and then move up to the bigger tables. Then win big again."

"Do you have enough time?"

I shrugged. "It depends on who's playing and for how much. Most of all, it depends on how the cards fall."

"So it's all luck?"

"No," I said. "It's skill, for sure. You play the cards, and you play the player. You play the odds, and you play the stacks. But, in the end, it all depends on how the cards fall. What the poker gods decide."

"Can I go with you?" she asked.

I hesitated. "I'd like that," I said slowly.

"But?"

I put my fork down and took a slug of coffee. "It might be distracting, is all. You're so..."

"So what?"

"So *you*."

She smiled, blushing slightly. "That's sweet, Casey."

"It's true."

"Well, what if I promise to be on my best behavior?"

"You're still gorgeous," I said. *And you fucking consume me.*

"I want to learn," she said. "I've tried it on my own at the low tables, but it's too slow going. I need to watch a professional. I need to watch you, Casey, and learn."

I didn't answer, just looked at her.

"I'll pay close attention," she promised. "We can talk later about the points I don't understand."

"I..."

"Just for a few hours," she said. "After that, I'll go practice on my own. I'll leave you alone."

"That's not what I meant. I—"

"I know. I didn't take it that way. But I get it. You're in a serious jam. You need to focus. But, so do I, or I'll never get my money back from that son of a bitch TV guy. Just let me watch for a couple of hours, and that's it. Then you can get done what you need to get done."

I thought about it for a few seconds, then nodded. "All right, Annie. You got it."

She smiled at me, and that smile made me feel better than when I'd won a championship. It had only been Double-A, after all.

I collected my cash from the cashier, and we strolled down the strip to the Cairo. After walking past King Tut and Cleopatra at the entrance, we made our way to the poker tables. I scanned the big game behind the velvet ropes.

"How much to sit?" I asked Carl, the security officer.

He cast an appraising eye on Annie, then looked at me and said, "More than you can handle, Casey."

"How much?"

"Buy-in is fifty."

Shit.

"Okay," I said. "I'll be back."

He didn't answer me.

We wandered through the tables until I found a mid-range table full of no one I knew except for Owen, the dealer. It seemed perfect, so I plopped down and waited out the hand. When an Arabic guy with red glasses raked in the modest pot, I put my cash on the table.

Owen counted the money in front of me, then announced that he was changing a thousand. The pit boss glanced over and nodded. Owen doled out my chips with expert fingers and dropped the cash down into the slot next to him.

I could feel Annie's warmth next to me as Owen dished the cards. I took a breath and tried to force myself into the zone. Feel that wave. Play the cards. Play the table.

Relax.

"Drink, sir?"

The waitress wore a tight skirt and a push-up bra, emphasizing her full breasts. I barely noticed.

"Water," I said, "with a wedge of lemon."

She smiled and strode away. I glanced at Annie, but she hadn't even seemed to acknowledge the waitress. Instead, she was staring at the table.

I turned to my cards, curling back the corners to peek.

Pocket nines.

It was a good start.

After an hour, I was up over eleven hundred, and two players had busted out and left the table. A heavyset man in a silky, salmon-colored dress shirt had taken one of the empty seats, but the other remained vacant.

We played on. Annie's presence didn't distract me like I thought it would. In fact, it seemed to be more like a good luck charm, as the cards fell for me almost exactly like I hoped they would. I even caught an open-ended ten-high straight on the river card, which ended up beating another player who had the bottom straight card.

My stacks grew. At least another hour passed, and I had to be at around four thousand total. I started to think about how much longer I should fleece these amateurs and build my stack before moving to a bigger table. If I could ride this wave long enough and at the right table, I could get to fifty and go sit at a table behind the velvet rope. My problem could be over tonight.

Owen dealt.

I checked my cards.

Queen of hearts. Queen of diamonds.

I wished I could smile, but this was poker.

Everyone checked around, with only two folds, so I went with the community consensus and checked, too. Owen flopped a seven, another queen, and a bullet.

Trips queens. I had to work this hand.

Another fold, a check and then a bet. I called and then raised modestly. Another fold, but two takers.

Owen burned and turned. A six.

I started running through the possibilities. There weren't many that could beat me, even if the river card went their way.

The man in the salmon-colored shirt bet five hundred. He was gunning for a straight, I figured. Possibly had an eight and a nine, or something like that. Or maybe he had a pocket pair, too. As long as they weren't aces, and as long as he didn't hit on the river, I was fine.

The Arabic guy in red glasses called, then pushed in another thousand.

Shit. Either he was bluffing, or he had the pocket aces.

Owen turned to me.

It was risky. Salmon could get his straight, if he was playing that. Or any pocket pair if the fourth card came up.

But the risk for my cards was the same for him, and for Arabic, too. Poker was a game of controlled risk. And I was in control, riding the wave.

Owen continued to stare at me, waiting. No pressure, not yet. I waited, letting the drama and the tension build. I could feel the warmth of Annie's body just inches away from me. I breathed in, searching for her scent in the middle of that casino aroma. I caught a wisp of her perfume, heady and strong, but subtle.

"We must call for you time?" the Arabic man asked in clipped English.

I smiled tightly and took a sip of my lemon water. "All in," I said, pushing my chips forward.

There were only a few people watching, but a soft murmur

went through the group. Annie's hand lighted on my shoulder, her nail raking across my skin in something akin to a caress.

Arabic frowned at the bet, biting his lip. Then he shrugged and pushed in his chips. "Call."

Salmon stared at me for a long while, fiddling with a chip, rolling it through his fat fingers. I gave him the flat stare I'd been perfecting for years, telling him nothing. Let him play the stacks, let him play the cards, but he wasn't going to play me.

"Time?" Arabic asked after a while.

"Let him have all time he wants," I said evenly.

Arabic scowled but left it alone.

Finally, Salmon set the chip down. "Call," he said.

Owen waited until he slid his chips forward. Then he announced that the pot was correct.

"You show?" Arabic asked, lifting his cards in preparation.

It was good form to show at times like this. Almost expected, really. Only an asshole said no. Still, I thought about it. My hesitation was more because I didn't want to know until that final card fell whether I'd bet their hands correctly.

Plus, this Arabic fuck was pushy, and I was tired of being pushed.

"No," I said. "I'm not showing."

"Pussy," Arabic said. "You are pussy."

Owen raised his hand before the guy was even finished saying the word for a second time. A shaven-headed, muscle-bound bull of a man appeared at the table before I could think of a response to Arabic.

"Problem, sir?" he asked politely.

No one answered. The bull crossed his massive arms and waited.

"So, we're not showing, then?" Salmon asked, his tone smooth. A smile played on his lips, and he was turning a chip in his fat fingers again.

"No," I said.

He shrugged, put down the chip, and turned over his own

cards.

Ace of clubs. Ace of hearts.

My blood froze, and my stomach clenched. Annie's hand fell away from my shoulder. I reached for my water and sipped. I heard Arabic mutter something that was probably a curse in his language.

"Fine," Arabic said. "I show."

I didn't want to look, but I had to. He rolled over a five and an eight, suited.

Shit. He was searching for that river card on an open-ended straight. There were still eight cards in that deck that would help him beat me.

But Salmon already had me beat.

Fuck.

There was one card in that deck that I needed. Another six or a seven didn't help me, even though it made a full boat. Salmon's boat was aces over. So I had one shot.

One.

The queen of spades. The Black Bitch. If she was in there. If she hadn't been in one of the hands that threw in earlier or one of the burn cards. What were the odds?

The odds were shit. But that didn't matter, because I was all in now.

Both of the players were staring at me. So were the people around the table. It seemed like there were twice as many in the crowd as there were before I went all in. The spotlight was on me. Everyone wanted to see my cards.

I shook my head. "Deal," I said.

Someone in the crowd muttered "asshole" but I ignored it. I watched Owen's hands as he burned a card and flipped over the river card.

The queen of spades stared up at me.

"Show!" Arabic nearly shouted.

I stared down at that last queen.

"Your cards, sir?" Owen asked politely.

Mechanically, I turned over my pocket queens. A light roar went up from the small, assembled crowd. Arabic and Salmon both cursed at the same time. One of them slapped the table, making the chips jump a little. Owen used a stick to push the large pile in the center of the table toward me.

"Congratulations," he said.

I barely noticed. I just stared back at the Black Bitch. Her enigmatic eyes gazed up at me, taking no pleasure in being my savior.

I turned to say something to Annie, but she had slipped away and was gone.

SIXTEEN
Cord

The phone chirp scares the bejesus out of me.

"Cord, me."

"Yeah, hey."

"I've decided I'm going to meet Babe Parcella alone. If he gets all pouty that you're not there, too, well, then he can just kiss my ass."

"You sure, man?"

"Double sure. There's no reason for you to have to be there. I think Parcella is going to play this like I said. Try to be our best buddies, offer to get rid of the threat, but then have his hand out, too. And he'll try to string it out."

"I'll be there if you want me. You know that. I'd be lying, though, if I said I *want* to be there, but you say the word and I'm right beside you."

"No way, muchacho. The more Babe gets you involved with this thing, the better it is for his future earnings. The less you are involved, the better for us."

"You still worried?"

"Yep. Babe said this blackmailer told him some things that were not ever mentioned by the Mexican cops or that ever got into any stories."

"Like?"

"The knife wounds on each body, this guy says they were

caused by two different knives."

"The other one that they never did and never will find?"

"Right."

"Well, yeah, that doesn't sound like a random threat. Sounds like somebody that might know something. What else?"

"I told you all of this last night...and I gotta get going anyway."

"Look, Ronnie. I, no, make that *we*, drank enough booze last night to float Noah's ark again. Hell, I don't remember my middle name right now."

"Ryan."

I take a big swig of orange juice, only because I had already drank the entire pot of coffee they had brought up.

"Whatever. Tell me again, son."

"He said that the cops couldn't understand how the big guy got so beat up. The other guy did it and *then* got butchered? The two girls?"

"Shit."

"Yeah. Shit. Anyway, he said he's going to tell us everything today. Well, he can tell me, not us. Meeting is at three. Downstairs in that big espresso café...The Lemon Tree, or whatever cutesy-ass name it is. He wanted to meet in his office, but I didn't like that. Didn't like it at all."

"Last chance, you want me there?"

"I'll call you after the meeting, pardner."

"I'll be seeing Annie this afternoon and tonight, but call me anyway."

"I will. Seeya."

Like I said, I'd be lying if I said I wasn't relieved about this. I got a great poker face, but that's when I'm playing cards. This meeting would not be about cards.

I tell myself Ronnie would handle it. Ronnie always handles it.

***

"What's wrong? Hey, hey, what's this?"

I'm walking from the bathroom and headed back to bed. I don't know if I have anything left, but I'm a gamer.

I look at the clock, and it's only like nine thirty or so. Some folks downstairs haven't even started the night at a table yet.

There is a soft lamp on by the bed. The only other lights are the Vegas casinos and just a dark purple hue in the west where the sun has disappeared. The drapes are pulled wide open, and the view is spectacular.

Her bare back is to me, and the sheet is down to the rise of her hip. Man, what a shape she has. Like a slim hourglass.

I had heard a little whimper, but it cut off as soon as I came out of the bathroom. Her shoulder is moving up and down a little.

"Annie, what is it? I mean, okay, I'm not twenty anymore, but I'm doing my best. Was it really *that* bad?"

No response. Sometimes humor works and sometimes it don't.

I'm standing here like the bed has suddenly turned into a minefield. I walk around it slowly.

Her shoulder is still moving softly. As I come around to the side of the bed she's facing, I can see that she's crying. Not a sound now, just big tears.

She holds a hand up and toward me, and when she does, I see her perfect shape from the front this time. I don't know, maybe it's all this other shit about Aruba going on, maybe it's me losing this Vegas tourney, or maybe it's all her. Whatever it is, what I'm looking at right now, tears included, I could happily just drown in. Just jump right in and fade away. What I'm feeling is something I've never felt. Not even close.

If she doesn't come to Atlantic City, fuck it, I'm going to California with her for a while. While I know that thought is crazy and I'm just all ga-ga right now, just *having* that thought makes me smile. Girl's got something over me, no doubt.

I look down at her and take her hand. It's warm and soft and silky, just like every damn inch of her.

Meanwhile, I'm smiling and she's crying. Great.

"Annie, sorry. Bad joke. What's wrong, darlin'?"

Another thing hits me just then. I actually care about what is wrong. Been a long dry spell for that kind of feeling.

She looks at me with those big, opal-green eyes and then her look slides back to the glass wall facing the western sky again.

"So beautiful." Her voice is a whisper.

I take another look too, for a moment, and then come right back to her. Quick. I kneel down at the bed and put my hand on her delicate chin. It is wet and trembling.

She smiles sadly but keeps looking at the dark sky.

I run my hand down slowly from her chin, down her neck, and over one perfect breast. Following that sleek shape, I slow even more over the rise of her hip and down to her thigh. Damn.

"Annie, tell me what you're thinking about."

"Cord, I can't. Not right now. It's not your problem."

"If you have a problem, I have a problem. Tell me. I mean that."

She looks at me and smiles that sad smile again. Her eyes though, her eyes are different. Almost shining now. Hungry.

I squeeze her hip gently and rubbed.

She shifts then and covers my hand with hers, moving it up to her breast.

She isn't smiling anymore, and her eyes slowly shut. Her mouth opens just a little and she sighs softly.

"Again, Cord. Again."

Her body is so warm, it's almost feverish.

"Right now."

This time is not like the first two slow-motion marathons. It is short, urgent, and borderline rough.

It isn't quiet either.

Like a brief, violent thunderstorm.

When the fight is over, I let out a little, winded chuckle. "Babe Parcella is probably on his way up here with a security team. I haven't made that much noise since I pulled a hamstring ten years ago."

She looks down at me and finally chuckles. A little bit. Her small hands move from my shoulders to my cheek, and then she comes down to rest on my chest.

"I know we talked about slowing down and letting this play out. But after the drive around town, the movie this afternoon and the great dinner tonight, I'm sure not sorry. This is perfect." I say it before I knew I was going to...and I don't care.

"This has been the best day of my life, Cord. I wouldn't change a thing, including right here, right now. I've never felt anything even close to what I've felt today...or tonight."

I reach for the room phone on the night table next to the bed.

"You like some Champagne?"

"Well, sure but—"

"Hey, 'sure but' nothing. We need to celebrate. Celebrate finding each other."

I tell the gal on the phone to send a bottle of their very best. That's a pretty serious order at the Magnum. She confirms the price to me. Just under six hundred Franklins.

"Ya'll ought to be ashamed of yourself, but send it on up with some other jazz to nibble on. Plenty of ice in that bucket now."

"Cord, you're crazy...and wonderful," Annie says from behind me.

"Thank you on both of those." I roll back and face her. "All I can tell you is it isn't Dom, but it is French. Louis something-something and it's 2001."

She laughs, but the smile only lasts a second.

My phone chirps on the dresser. It's probably Ronnie. He hasn't called me yet from this afternoon's talk with Parcella.

"Be right back."

I get up and head for the bathroom. There's a hotel robe in there. On the way, I snag the phone on the fourth ring.

"Cord speakin'."

I keep going and throw the robe on. I never wear these damn things, but that champagne won't take long. They're pretty damn quick here, depending on who you are, what floor you're on.

"Hey, pardner." Ronnie sounds more in the bag than I was. Annie and I had already put away some wine at dinner.

"You sound tired or drunk. Which one?"

"Both. Listen, everything is going to be all right. I won't get into it much, but we're fine. I also kinda sent Parcella a few messages to butt the fuck out."

"You sure?"

"Yeah. Yeah, I'm sure."

I walk back into the room and hand Annie a robe, too.

The phone line is quiet now.

"Hello? Ronnie?"

"She's there, right?"

"Right." I switch into secret-man talk mode. Turning around, I pace around a little. "So, you sure you didn't lose all our money?"

"I'll tell you the rest tomorrow. Lunch, okay? One, two o'clock. Upstairs in the good restaurant. I want something good. I need to see you alone, though."

"We're good, though?"

"Yeah, we're good."

He clicked off.

It's my turn to stand and stare out the window. Didn't like the way he sounded.

Two arms circle my waist from behind.

I turn to her and she looks so good in that oversized robe... that isn't cinched up. Damn if she isn't crying again, though.

"Annie?"

"Is everything okay?"

"Yeah, that was Ronnie. We're working through a little problem ourselves."

She nods sadly and then does her best to smile up at me. It doesn't work out too well and she buries her face in my chest.

I take her by the hand and walk her into the living area. There's some nice comfortable chairs and a kickass couch. I get her seated on the couch, and then I sit down too, sliding an arm around her waist.

"Okay, look. This is coming out right now." I look at her and raise her chin with my hand. "This thing I got going on is fine now, and it probably never did measure up to whatever it is you got going on."

She just gives me those green eyes and blinks.

"I..."

"Annie, I'm just gonna keep asking and bothering you until you tell me. So, what is it? Whatever it is, I'll understand."

"Oh, I don't think so. It's serious stuff."

"Let me tell you something, punkin', you wouldn't believe what it would take to shock me."

"Let's just have a good rest of the night."

"We will. After you tell me what's going on." I drop my hand away from her chin and stand up. "Okay now, it stops here. Take it from the beginning. I mean it, Annie. I can help."

She looks at me and then looks down to her lap.

"First, I don't expect anything, Cord. I'm just telling you what's going on and what's bothering me. That's it."

I just nod and put my arm around her again. She's going now, and I'm not ruining the momentum by running my mouth.

"I'm so ashamed."

I smile and give her hand a squeeze. Right now, she could tell me she killed her sister this morning and I'd smile and nod.

"Well okay, okay. The other day, when we played cards against each other? And I kept playing even though you said to stop?"

"Right." I don't smile. Joke time is over.

"Well, that whole time or almost all of it, I was playing on that asshole's money. Like a fool. Like a fool, I played on his money. He put a couple of rolls of money in my purse when I came back from the bathroom and he was headed to it. Remember when I left for the bathroom? He, he said 'take this and beat his ass.' He told me hated you and said he wanted to see you get beat. Said he could beat you easy but he was having a run of bad cards all day. He said he had no luck going on, but I did...."

Once she starts, the words just come. Fast.

"What else happened? Because so far, all I need to do is kick his ass. Cory, or Casey, right?"

She takes a deep shuddering breath, and I can tell it's going to come out again in a rush.

"He was so nice when I met him that first day in town. Showed me around, he never tried anything. It was all just natural. When we were playing cards, before you got there, I got hot and won a lot. But I'm no good, Cord. You tried to tell me that, but I thought I was good. Thought I was real good. Anyway, he wanted his money back from me. All of it. He keeps threatening me, calling me, following me over at the Riv. I tried to win it back at the tables the last two days, but I can't win. I just can't win enough. Not nearly enough."

Gasping for air now, breaking into sobs, she puts her hands to her face and looks down again.

If he was in the room right now, this Casey ass wouldn't stand a chance. Man, I wish he was here...

"Annie...Annie, this thing is going to be all right, hon. You just got caught up in things, that's all. I'll help you with the money, babe. I don't know how much it was now, but it wasn't something I can't handle pretty easy. Money is only money, darlin'."

She sobs again and shakes her head back and forth. She doesn't stop, shaking faster.

"Not good enough anymore. He won't take the money anymore. He called me this morning. Says I have until noon tomorrow to set it up. Says I'll never see California if I don't swing it."

"What? Don't swing what?"

She takes a deep breath.

Then she looks at me with red eyes and a tear-stained face. It's the most terrified look I've ever seen someone have.

"He says he knows people in this town who will kill somebody for almost nothing. Cord, I'm so scared."

"Okay, Annie, it's okay. What's he want now? Just tell me what he wants."

She sighs and looks over my shoulder for a moment but then comes back to my eyes. She puts a soft hand to my cheek.

"He wants a private card game with you. In a private game suite, here at the Magnum. Says he'll leave me alone and we're all square if I can get it done...told me he'll enjoy kicking your ass, and if you pussy out, like he thinks you probably will...they'll never find me otherwise."

"Annie, you're going to Atlantic City with me."

"I'm not doing that to you, Cord. Not with all of this baggage. He said he'd find me wherever I went, anyway. He knows some very bad people."

"Fuck him and his bad people. Tell him to challenge me, then. We'll see who the pussy is."

"I won't let you play this bastard, so I'm leaving early morning tomorrow for California. I have to try. I just can't live like this anymore."

"You're not going anywhere in the morning."

I decide quickly. She did owe him money. He probably is a half-crazy bastard and it sure explained the way he acted after the game. I took that asshole's money, not Annie's. I'll take it again, too. It'll be better than if I'd won this tournament.

What the hell, if I do lose, which I won't, big fuckin' deal. Of course, Ronnie will really be pissed when I tell him. He'll have a shit fit. But hey, won't be the first time for that. Despite everything, I smile at that.

The door buzzes. Champagne's here.

I pull her face up and smile at her.

"Annie, this is nothing. It's all good. I'll take care of the game. We'll do it here at the Magnum. I'll work it out. Casino rules, dealer, the whole bit."

"Oh Cord...no, I..."

"Sorry. Done deal. I won't have it any other way. Fucker will sign a debt paid note, too."

She starts to tear up again, but I don't think there are any more left in her.

"Give me a smile now. A real one."

She jumps up into my arms instead.

"Well hell, I can't see now. Are you smiling? That's all I want."

I laugh, and it feels good.

She takes a couple of hitched breaths and then laughs a little too.

The door buzzes again.

"Well, I'm thirsty, but I'm not letting go of you."

I throw her upwards a little and hold her tight as I start walking towards the door. She wraps her legs around my waist and off we go.

"Cord, don't ever leave me. Promise me that."

What a day, what a night. Lucky in cards and lucky in love, I guess.

SEVENTEEN
Casey

Annie found me at the twenty-five dollar Let It Ride table sometime well after breakfast. She looked tired, and a little drawn, but still more gorgeous than ninety-eight percent of the women on this planet. I figured with three hours of sleep, she'd put the other two to shame, too.

"Where'd you go?" I asked.

"Did you catch the river card?"

"Yeah," I said, nodding. "Queen of spades. The black bitch."

"I *knew* you'd win that hand."

"Why'd you leave?" I asked again. "After I won, I looked for you, but you were gone."

She gave me a sad smile. "That was your moment, Casey."

I wanted to say that it was a moment I would have liked to have shared with her, but I just looked at her foolishly.

She smiled wider. "Remember what you told me? About riding the wave?"

I blushed a little, glancing up at the bored dealer. She stared at me without expression, waiting for me to decide on my bet. I'd caught a pair of tens in my hand, so I was in the money no matter what happened. I slid my cards under my chips and gave her a wave to let it ride. I made sure to use my right hand, keeping my bandaged left out of sight. I was tired of people staring at it. Some even asked questions.

I turned back to Annie and lowered my voice. "We don't talk about that kind of stuff out in the open," I said.

"It's embarrassing?"

"It's bad luck."

"Oh." She lowered her voice to a stage whisper. "So, I shouldn't talk about what you did to me in the chair by the window, either, huh?"

I blinked. I opened my mouth to say something, but nothing came out. Beautiful women rarely had that effect on me, but then this girl was something different. And a little dangerous.

"Winner," my dealer announced blandly.

I looked at her hand. A third ten turned up, giving me trips tens. Then I noticed her other card was a four, which matched the four in my hand.

A full boat.

The dealer turned on the flashing red light. Thankfully, she didn't hit the music button that some dealers did, at least during prime time. The pit boss wandered over, verified the hand and my bonus bets.

"Pay all," was all he said.

The dealer started stacking chips. I quickly did the math out of habit. Eight twenty-five on the bet, another twenty-five on the bonus for my hand, and four hundred for the one-dollar bonus bet…twelve hundred and fifty dollars.

"Still riding the wave," Annie said with a sly smile. Then her face turned into an exaggerated pout. "Does that mean you're staying at the table for a while longer, or…?"

I smiled, tempted. I'd seen some wild times in the sack, especially back in my playing days, but no one matched the intensity or the deep mystery of Annie. When I was with her, it seemed like the rest of the world faded into nothing.

But I was winning. And I needed to get my ass to the big tables, where I could turn this money into the kind that saved my ass from the Swede.

"I thought you wanted to learn this game."

"Let It Ride?"

I snorted. "No. This is just a time passer. I meant poker."

"I know. Just playing with you." She nudged me with her hip, jamming right into my bandaged hand.

Fiery pain shot through every nerve in my left arm. I winced and bit back a yell.

"Oh! I'm so sorry!" She reached down and took my wrist. "Your poor hand, baby. I wish I could kiss it."

Corny as it sounded, I kinda wished it, too.

"Come on," I said, raking in all my chips and tossing a twenty-five to the stoic dealer. "Let's go over to—"

"Casey?" A familiar voice came from behind me.

I turned and there was Nicky.

We stared at each other for a long minute. I tried to decide how to react. This wasn't the first time I'd been caught with another woman, though not with Nicky. Even so, I didn't rattle easily. Kept a poker face. The problem was, this was the first time the woman who caught me was a cop.

"Hey," I finally managed.

"Hey?" she asked, her expression a combination of anger and incredulity. "That's the best you can do?"

"I didn't expect to see you," I said lamely.

Her gaze flicked to Annie and then back to me. "Yeah, I kinda figured that. Who's the bimbo?"

I looked at Annie involuntarily, but she kept her cool. Her green eyes stared back at Nicky's deep brown ones, her expression even flatter than my dealer's had been.

"Uh, this is Annie. We were just playing some Let It Ride."

She snorted. "Nice one." She shook her head. "You know I've spent the past two days worried about you? Wondering what the fuck was up? What a waste of time."

Annie stepped back slowly. "I'm going to go. It's obvious you two need to talk..."

"No," Nicky said coldly. "Don't bother, Barbie. You can have him."

"It's not what you think."

"Bitch, you don't even begin to know what I *think*."

"I'm sorry," Annie said quietly and slipped away.

Nicky's gaze followed her, then returned to me. "How long has this been going on?"

I shook my head. "There's nothing going on. I was playing cards. She was playing cards." I turned to the dealer for confirmation, but she gave me a look that said there was no way she was lying for a measly twenty-five-dollar tip. I looked back at Nicky. "Really, Nicky. We—"

"Are obviously fucking," Nicky said. "And don't give me this shit about playing cards. You think I just now bumped into you? I've been standing over there for ten minutes. I saw her walk up, and I saw how you looked at her and..." she trailed off, shaking her head. "Why am I bothering talking to you?" She raised her hands in front of her and waved them back and forth. "It's over."

"Nicky, wait." I reached out with both hands as she was turning away. My left hand smacked the table, and I let out a loud grunt of pain.

She stopped and gave me another look. "What the fuck happened to your hand?"

"Nothing," I said.

"Casey, what—"

"I thought you were done with me," I said, the pain in my hand fueling my anger. "So go."

She pressed her lips together in a tight frown. Then, quicker than I could react, she reached out and grabbed my right hand. A moment later, she had me in a wrist lock. She bent it hard enough to get me up on my toes.

"Ow, goddamnit! What are you—"

"This way," she ordered in her lieutenant voice. She half escorted, half dragged me from the table and down the aisle.

"Fuck, Nicky. You're hurting my wrist."

"Then stop resisting."

"Stop *resisting*? What the hell are you doing?"

"Getting to the bottom of this bullshit."

"Jesus, Nicky. Let me go."

She answered me by ratcheting up the wristlock just a notch. I struggled to walk along with her determined stride, half up on my tiptoes, my teeth grinding together. People looked up from their gaming tables, showing mild interest for a moment, then turning back.

"Ow! Fuck!"

"Stop being a pussy."

I changed tactics. "We gotta go back. That's my money on the table."

"They'll keep it there."

I stopped talking. A minute later, we were in the security station. The casino security guy rose in his chair, but then he saw the flash of her badge on her belt next to the gun, or maybe just the fire in her eyes. Either way, he sat back down.

"Holding One open?" Nicky growled out the question.

He nodded wordlessly.

Nicky opened the door with my face, then used her leverage to send me staggering into the far wall. She closed the door behind her.

I shook my hand, working the soreness out of my wrist. "That fucking hurt."

"Oh, and seeing you with some little fuck toy in the casino, that felt good?"

"She's not—"

"Save it," she interrupted. She pointed at my bandaged hand. "Talk."

I sat down in one of the chairs, adjusting it to buy some time. Nicky sensed lies that I even thought, much less those I might tell. I'd never been able to bullshit her once she turned her sights on me. If she hadn't been so caught up in work these past few weeks, I know she would have ferreted out my situation with the Swede. But she was too busy trying to tie Babe Parcella into something nasty.

"I think you sprained my wrist," I said.

"The hand," she repeated, no mercy or remorse in her tone.

I gave her an even gaze. "I cut it chopping tomatoes for a salad, okay? It took a few stitches. No big deal."

"Bullshit."

"True." I made a clumsy cross with my right hand. "God's honest."

"So now you're Catholic? That's convenient."

I shrugged.

She stared at me. "I don't know why I should even care." She shook her head at me. Her eyes were full of anger and something else. Hurt? Disappointment? I couldn't tell.

"Because you don't want to be alone," I said, softening my voice a little. "And neither do I."

"That's obviously not a problem for you," she said.

I sighed. "Nicky...really. It was a little harmless flirtation. She came onto me. I just—"

"Is everything you say a lie?"

I fell silent.

"Really," she said. "I want to know. Because if it is, then logic would tell me that everything you *ever* said is a lie, too."

"No..." I whispered.

"Which means I just spent the last two years wasting my time, just fucking some mope who wasn't even faithful to me."

I shook my head again, this time with less conviction. She was starting to piss me off. "Nicky..."

"You could have just told me up front," she said, ignoring my protest. "If all it was going to be was some occasional, piss-poor sex, hell, I was desperate enough at the time that I would have went even for that. But you didn't have to pretend it was anything more than that. That shit's cold."

"Cold?" I raised my eyebrows. "You want to talk cold? How about trying to get close to someone who thinks about her fucking job twenty-four seven? How would you like to always be second place to that?"

"At least you were never second place to some blonde slut," Nicky shot back.

"She's not a slut."

"Oh..." Nicky nodded. "I see. Defend the slut's honor. I get it. She's special or something, right?"

I swallowed and looked away. I didn't want it to end this way, but I could see that it was probably going to do just that, whether I wanted it or not. She was right about Annie and me fucking and about her being special. So what else was there?

"You know how much I risked to be with you?" she asked quietly.

"Nothing," I said, "except your career."

"Which is all I got."

"Exactly," I agreed, looking up again. I met her eyes without shame or regret. "You think you're hot shit, Nicky, but you know what? You're not so smart. You don't know nearly half as much as you think you do."

"I know enough to catch your cheating white ass."

"Oh, so now it's a white and black thing?"

"It sure seems to be, considering the little Barbie doll you obviously prefer."

I shook my head. "That's got nothing to do with it."

"Bullshit."

"True."

"You're so full of shit, Casey."

"No, it's true. You know why it's her now and not you? I'll tell you why. You want to know?"

"Go ahead," she said. "Lay it out there, big man."

"She's *here*," I said, pointing my finger into the palm of my hand. "Not somewhere else all the time."

"Oh, that's fucking rich. You tell yourself that, if it helps you sleep. I'm done with this, and you." She turned to go.

"You were right about Parcella," I said after her, quietly.

She stopped. Her head turned slowly until her eyes locked warily onto mine. "The fuck you talking about?"

"He's dirty," I told her. "He staked me cash."

"He's stake-horsing?" she asked. That was illegal if you were a licensed security director, but no one ever bothered with it.

"No," I said. "He gave it to me with points. Straight up shylock."

Her jaw dropped. "You're shitting me."

"Nope."

"I was fucking right." Her eyes looked past me at the wall, gears grinding. I almost smiled at the irony. Even when she was here with me, she wasn't really here.

"That's not the half of it. He does business with the Swede. Sells him loans."

"The Swede? How...how do you know this?"

"Shit." I laughed.

"How? Tell me!"

"Everyone knows it," I exaggerated. "Except the cops."

"How do you know?" she repeated.

"Because he sold my loan to the Swede."

"Your...your loan? What loan? I..."

"Don't have a clue? Because you're never here, like I said?" I nodded. "Yeah, I know."

She shook her head and her eyes snapped into focus, drilling into me. "What loan? How much?"

"More than you make in a year," I said.

Her jaw dropped again. "You owe the Swede..."

"Yeah. That much."

"And Babe is...?"

"Small time, but in it, yeah." I held up my left hand. "And this wasn't from cutting tomatoes for a salad. It was a warning from the Swede that he was serious about me paying him back."

"He broke your finger?"

"He cut the tip off my finger."

Nicky blinked as if she couldn't rectify the words I spoke with what they meant. "Wait..."

"No," I said. "I'm done waiting. You want to break up. We're broke up. You can't help me with my problem, and I *am* your problem, so it's better this way, anyway."

"No," she said. "Now that you've told me about this, we can bring in the case. We can—"

I laughed. "You can't do shit, Nicky. Not you or anyone like you. Vegas is what Vegas is. You're trying to make it into something it's not, and you'll never be successful."

Tears sprang into her eyes. I'd finally hurt her enough to get that response. All it took was to call her career futile.

"We—"

"There is no we," I said. "I only told you all this so you'd understand. It's not like I'll testify to any of it. I just want you to know what a waste all that effort you put into Parcella really was. You and I never stood a chance against all of that, and now all of that isn't going to amount to shit. It's a damn shame and a waste."

"No, it's...I'll...we'll..."

"Like I said, there's no we. There's you and there's me. And I'm leaving." I stood up and walked toward the door.

When I was almost past her, she reached out and caught me by the upper arm. "I'll have you subpoenaed, Casey," she said, her composure creeping back in. "I'll get the prosecutor to put you on the stand, and if you don't tell me everything, it'll be perjury."

"Says who? You and all your witnesses?" I shook my arm free. "Good luck with that."

I walked out, not giving the security guard a glance as I left the room and headed back into the casino.

I had to find Annie. I was all in now.

She didn't answer her phone. I didn't bother with a message. After I cashed in my chips from the Let It Ride table and called her again, she answered.

"I'm in the bar across the street."

"At the Bellagio?"

"No, the little dive next to Margaritaville."

I knew the place but forgot the name. It didn't matter. She was seated in the front corner and waved at me through the window. I slid into the booth across the table from her. Before either of us could say a word, the waitress appeared. She gave me an expectant look.

I motioned toward Annie's drink. "Whatever she's having."

The waitress turned to Annie.

"Rum and coke," Annie said.

The waitress shuffled way.

Annie ignored her. "Everything all right?" she asked.

I shrugged. "It was never all right."

"I didn't mean to be the reason for something breaking up," she said. "If I'd have known—"

"It's been over for a while," I said. "I think we both knew it. It was just too much work to call it out."

She nodded as if she understood. Hell, she probably did.

"Anyway," I said, "it doesn't matter. What matters is getting into one of those big games and winning. Then I can—"

"What if..." she started to say, then stopped and shook her head. "No, it's not your problem."

"What?"

"No, never mind. Finish telling me your plan."

"No," I said. "Tell me what you were going to say. What if what?"

She bit her lip, then took a sip of her drink. The waitress showed up with mine and slid it in front of me. I let it sit.

"What if what, Annie? Tell me."

She took another swallow of the rum and coke, then sighed. "I think I screwed up," she finally said.

"How?"

"I've been practicing at the small tables, you know?"

"Yeah. And?"

"And I thought I was getting better. Learning. So I put on my big girl panties, and I did it."

"Did what?"

"Challenged that son of a bitch who took my money."

"You challenged him?"

She bit her lip and nodded. "Yeah."

"When?"

"Last night. After I saw you win that hand, I just felt...I don't know...*alive*. Like anything was possible. So I called over to the Magnum and challenged him."

I shook my head in disbelief. "No way he accepted."

She nodded. "He did."

Christ.

"When? Where?"

"I don't know yet, but it'll be at the Magnum. In a private suite with a house dealer."

"Head to head? You challenged him head to head? For how much?"

"All of it," she whispered. "Everything I've got."

"Jesus."

"Afterward, after the excitement faded, I realized something." Big tears welled up in her eyes. She brushed them away, fought them back. "I realized that I couldn't beat him. He's a pro. I'm not."

She was right. He'd fleece her. Again.

"He's going to take everything," she said. "Everything."

"Don't show," I said. "Be a no-show. He can't force you to sit down."

Her eyes fell.

"No," I said. "Don't tell me..."

"I already gave the money to him."

"You just *gave* him the money?"

She nodded. "To show him I was serious."

"You better hope he doesn't just pocket it and say thank you, ma'am."

She frowned. "I don't think he'd do that. Besides, he said he'd get someone neutral to stand in and watch. Plus, his manager will be there."

"Fucking Christ on a popsicle stick, Annie. You're walking into the lion's den there. You can't do it."

"I know."

"Then don't."

"I know *I* can't," she said.

I paused, letting what she said sink in. Then I asked her what she meant. I knew, but I wanted to hear her say it.

She did.

"I want you to be my champion, Casey. Get my money back. When you do, I'll give you whatever you need to pay off the gangster that you owe. We'll both get a fresh start."

I wanted to say that maybe we'd get that fresh start together, but there'd be time for that part after. After I carved this cowpoke's heart out and fed it to him.

"I'll do it," I said.

"Really?"

"Yeah. But a couple of conditions first."

"Anything."

"You call him back and tell him that if his punk manager is going to be there, I want a second, too."

"A second?"

"A friendly witness. You."

"Ah. Got it."

"And I pick the dealer. I want Tala. She works at the Magnum."

"Why her?"

"She won't give us any help other than to deal it straight. That's the best you can hope for in a game like that."

She looked at me, nodding that she understood.

I sighed. "I'd like to pick the proctor, too, but if I'm picking the dealer, I suppose that's up to him."

"That would seem fair."

"Fuck fair," I muttered. "We shouldn't be doing this."

But my mind was already turning. This was what we should be doing. One game, in private, and when I win, all my problems with the Swede are over. And even if I lose, no one will know about it for a while. I won't have Mats or some other thug standing at my elbow in the open casino while we play.

"Thank you," she said, smiling. Her smile made the world seem all right for just a few seconds. Then she leaned across the table and kissed me lightly on the corner of my mouth.

I should be thanking you, I thought. *You're a goddamn angel. An angel of deliverance.*

"Thank you," she whispered again.

"Don't thank me yet," I said. "I haven't won shit."

"You will," she said. "I know you will."

EIGHTEEN
Cord

"You did what?"

"Taped it."

"Well, well, well. You sneaky bastard."

I shake my head and smile at him. Only Ronnie.

He just gives me a half smile and then shovels in some more of his omelet. Biggest omelet I've ever seen, too.

He looks bad, and he never looks bad, even after hanging with me all night after some big bender. He is always up first, looking fresh and wondering why everybody else looks like shit.

Not today.

It's a little past noon, which is damn early for me, and I'm all about the coffee right now. My stomach is grumbling, though, so it won't be long.

The opulent Parisian serves an outstanding brunch as well as high-dollar dinners, so you don't find any mopes up here slamming something called the All American plate.

This is expensive whale territory; there are only four other parties scattered around the large room. We're only about three tables over from where Annie and I had dinner that first time.

I hold up my cup to a waiter about a mile away, but he still sees me instantly.

"Hey, I wasn't messin' around." Ronnie wipes off the corners of his mouth with a napkin and then put it back on his lap.

"Have I told you look like shit this morning?"

"Three times now." A big piece of bacon he's holding disappears. "At least I got an excuse, ass face."

I'm watching him as he wades through the meal. Another bite of the oversized English muffin, a crystal goblet of orange juice gets drained, then another forkful of omelet.

"Are you getting executed this afternoon or what?"

"Anyway." He takes what kind of looks like a little cell phone out, but it isn't, and sets it on the table. "One reason was to have a little insurance. I'm pretty sure casino security chiefs aren't supposed to do this kind of thing, right? The other was to save me the trouble of repeating all of this horseshit or forgetting something."

I hadn't been paying attention and, out of nowhere, the waiter is walking up behind Ronnie.

"Mr. Needham? The same Kona blend?" The waiter is holding a pot and smiles.

"Oh, *hell* yes, Javier. Some of the best damn coffee I've had here. And hey, can I get the exact same thing that my death row friend is having here for his last meal?"

"Of course." He's smiling as he leans in and pours me another cup. "I'll put the order in right away. Mr. Turnbull, more coffee or juice?"

"I think I'm good. Thanks."

Javier walks away, and I look down at the small recorder. It's razor thin.

"Where the hell did you get that thing?"

"I've had it for a while but never used it."

He reaches over and looks at the volume, making sure it's low. "If someone starts walking up to us from behind me again, just wave at them so I'll know."

He flips it on and then turns the volume just a little lower. There is about a three-second pause, then, "Great to see you again. Enjoying your stay?"

Babe Parcella's voice is low and deep. I look at Ronnie and

smile. My ear is cocked downward like a dog.

"You bet."

"Excellent. Okay, so good, good. Well listen, I know you're busy, and I am too, so here it is in a nutshell. This guy said he would be in contact with you soon..."

There was another voice, but I couldn't hear it. Female. Then Babe again, "No thanks Lori, no I don't need anything. Nope."

A pause, just background noise.

"Anyway, he said for me to tell you this was the real deal and that you might want to think about pulling out of Atlantic City. Told me to relay this so you'd know he wasn't some crackpot, and he wasn't fucking around."

"Why you Mr. Parcella?"

"Ronnie, look, please call me Babe."

"Sure."

"This guy used to work for me. He knows that I have all kinds of access to things and people."

"Why you s'pose he did that, though, instead of just coming to us with the phone call?"

"I guess he figured that I would know how to get a hold of you and let you know right away. Wanted to amp up the pressure maybe, I dunno. I don't really know, Ronnie."

"It's been four years. The Mexican cops can't find their own asshole this afternoon, let alone four years ago. Where's he been?"

"That's what I thought, too, but he's been in prison. The guy is out now. He's Mexican, too, and knows people down there."

"What else did he want you to do besides be the middle man in this shakedown?"

Ronnie reaches over and stops the recorder. "His expression and manner changed right there. Stared at me real hard and leaned in on me."

He turns it back on, and Babe's voice continues. "Mr. Turnbull, I understand your concern and suspicions about this. I'm telling you all this in good faith. I'm on your side here."

"Babe, please, call me Ronnie. Easy. Actually, that's not what

I meant at all. I meant did he try to threaten *you* or ask you to do anything dangerous? You're being awful defensive all of a sudden. No need."

"Well, thanks, Ronnie. Appreciate the thought. I just feel uncomfortable about this whole thing, and I'm concerned. You and Cord are good people."

"Okay, well, first of all, thanks for seeing me and letting me know about this mysterious...*guy*."

"Hey, if I knew where he was, I'd have some people go talk to him about pulling me into this. Not so nice people."

"Second thing is, it's all bullshit. We were never even on that beach that night. We were with my brother and his wife after the hotel bar closed. Watched the sun come up with them. We were stinking drunk out on their balcony."

"Like I told you, this guy says the Mexican cops never believed your brother when they interviewed him. They also never understood the big guy being so beat up and the knife wounds thing."

"Yeah, I hear you. All I can say is this guy that called you has got shit. Nothing."

"What about this guy still in prison who was convicted for it? My guy says he's crying about things now, says his memory is coming back."

"*Your* guy?"

"You know what I'm trying to say."

"Babe, seriously, it's all bullshit. I'm not worried, so you shouldn't be."

"Well, okay, but he told me an associate of his would call you. They'll state their demands. So, if I can be of any help, in any way, please let me know."

"I actually look forward to that call. In fact, here."

Another pause.

"Please give him this number. I always answer. I just mean, well, you know, if he happens to call you back."

"Again, my only concern here is you guys. My business is half security and half confidentiality, so please don't worry about that."

Ronnie looks at me, reaches over, and shuts the recording off again. "I gave him the 'I know you're full of shit' look right about here as I'm getting up and starting to leave."

"So, is he kind of floundering around right now or what?"

"Yeah, and I wanted him to feel a little uneasy about being involved. Having some skin in the game."

He flips it on again, and there was just some clinking restaurant noises going on for a few seconds.

"Right, right. Hell, I know that, Babe. I appreciate it, too. I really do. When this is done, we'll make sure your boss treats you right. Make sure he knows how much you've helped us."

Only thing I could hear now was rustling around and then from the distance, "Thanks, gentlemen."

Still nothing from Babe.

I thought the tape was over, and then I heard Ronnie in a quiet tone. "Oh, and hey, what's this guy's name, anyway? He worked for you, right? You never told me."

"Miguel Salazar. Whereabouts unknown, unfortunately. A bad dude, but if I find him…he'll wish he'd never made that call."

Ronnie turns it off and puts it in his pocket. He looks at me with a grim smile. "So, there you go, Cord."

"What are we going to do? I thought we were good on this?" I don't see how this is all good now.

"You didn't catch it?"

"Catch what?"

"When I walked away, I couldn't really believe it. I had no choice, though, I had to believe it."

"You lost me."

"Babe doesn't know this guy from Adam. The Mexican cops never even interviewed my brother in Aruba."

"So, what then, this Salazar guy is just lying?"

"Cord, there is no Salazar."

I just look at him for a moment trying to digest all of this. Then I remember us saying that there were only two people who really knew what happened that night.

One is a twice-convicted con that has brain damage and can't remember his own birthday. The other is, well, it's Ronnie's brother, Michael.

Ronnie is just looking at me. Sad look.

"Wait now. No way." I'm staring back at him.

"It's him, Cord. We were never that close to begin with. Older we got, the more he resented me. Resented us. When I didn't make it back for Paula's funeral, well that probably didn't set good with ol' Mikey. Just the last straw."

"Well, yeah, but...damn."

"Hey, it happens. He lost his job, lost his wife, and two new Jags. That house on the gulf coast that he was over his head on, anyway? Ain't near being paid for. The dumbass needs money. Like now."

"Have you two always been bad?"

"Pretty much. The reason he said he would step up for us in Aruba was basically only because of us being brothers. That's it."

"Why now?"

"He said he was watching the tournament and saw your grinning mug at the Magnum final table...then he—"

"You talked to him?"

"Yup, called him last night. Right after I spoke to you. While I could still put a sentence together. Busted his blackmailing little ass and he coughed."

Out of the corner of my eye, I see my meal coming. "Hold on."

Javier gets me all set up and squared away. "Okay, there we go. Anything else gentlemen?"

"That'll do it. Thanks, Javier."

"So, Cord, this is all on me, and I'm sorry." He looked away casually, but I could tell this was killing him.

"Hey, pard, it's me here...forget it. Main thing is we're good on this." I shrugged and waved a hand at him.

"He needs money, and I'm going to give him money. It will

always be out of my cut, though, so don't sweat that. Don't ever doubt that, Cord."

"Hey." I wave a hand in front of his face. "I said it's me here, bucky. I'd never think that."

"Anyway, this turned to be a big bunch of nothin', and we're good to go. I'm going to let that asshole Babe know that I took care of things and we don't need him. Make sure he knows I know about his little line of bullshit about Salazar, his made-up old employee."

"Alright then. Done."

We sit there for a minute, and I take a few bites. It hits me that there is no time like the present. The more I think about this, it's perfect, really.

"Remember I told you when I sat down that I had something I wanted to do before we leave for AC?"

"Yeah, whatcha got planned? Shoot."

"Well, I was thinking just now, how about giving your brother somebody else's money?"

He looks at me, then drinks the last of his ice water. "I don't like the sound of this already."

"I have a private game set up. No press, no crowd, private suite. One challenger."

"Who? You know our rules about this shit."

"I know, I know. This is something I need to do, though, and I'm going to do it. It's against that dickhead the other day, the one that got in my face."

"Really? Perfect. Oh, that's just perfect, Cord. What're you, fucking nuts?"

"All of this will be on the level. Private suite, right here at the Magnum, house dealer, house rules, security, the whole thing."

"All right now. Listen. I know something else is up here. Tell me now before I get up and start drinking again." He shook his head. "I mean it. You don't need to be doin' this kind of bullshit."

"You're right. I don't need to, but I've made my mind up. I'll use my own personal money, not team money."

"Like I've told you before, you're a big boy. I can't tell you what to do, but what is this, Cord?"

"Annie needs my help, and I'm gonna help her. This ass, this Casey guy, has been threatening her. She owes him money from the other day, but then he changed his debt demand. If she can get a game set up between him and me, she's off the—"

"Whoa, now. Just back the truck up, son. This thing smells."

"I'm not getting into it all because it just don't matter. Main thing is, I'm gonna get this guy off her ass for good."

Ronnie didn't say anything, he just kept staring.

"Hey, my money, Ronnie. Don't sweat it. After I kick his ass, I'll donate it to the Michael fund."

That didn't sound or work like I wanted it to.

Ronnie stood up to go. "Cord, at this point with all the bullshit going on with my brother, I just don't give a rat's ass about anything. So, have a ball."

"Ronnie, hold on. I'm sorry, that was a stupid thing to say. I just mean I'll kick the winnings over to you because I don't care about the money. I just want to whup this guy's ass."

He didn't walk away at least. Instead, he looked down at his feet. "When?"

"She called me just before I came up here to eat. Tonight or tomorrow night works. I'm supposed to call her back and tell her. After the game, we all head to Atlantic City and kick some more ass."

"You have this game all set up already? Damn Cord, you sure you want to do this?"

"Sure as rain, and no, as a matter of fact, I don't have it completely set up."

"Which means you don't have any of it set up?"

"Well, I have all the details."

I gave him a grin.

No charm there, either.

He's had enough, and he just walks away.

Then he stops with his back to me. Slowly, he turns and gives me a grin, walking back. "All right, you crazy bastard. I imagine after I have my little talk with Babe Parcella, he'll be willing to help with the setup."

"I think you're right, pardner." Ronnie can be vindictive as hell.

"You just said *we* all head to Atlantic City, didn't you?"

I decide to ignore that for now. "And hey, I need you at this private game, pardner. Can't win without you."

"You're such an unbelievable pain in the ass."

He's still smiling.

NINETEEN
Casey

"So, tonight?" I asked her.

We were lying on top of the covers in her room at the Riviera. The air conditioner hummed and blew cool air over our sweaty bodies. She had her head on my chest.

She nodded and caressed my hand. "Yeah. Well, in about an hour or so."

"Who called you?"

"Parcella. He's handling everything."

"He's a crooked motherfucker," I said, but not forcefully. "But I suppose there's nothing we can do about that choice."

"No," she said softly.

I could feel her confidence ebbing as the game drew closer. She was too sweet to say it, but it was written all over her face.

"Hey," I said, touching her cheek and turning her to face me. "It's going to be okay. I can beat him."

"He's a professional," she said.

"So am I."

"He's..." she trailed off, not saying it.

"A real professional?" I asked.

"That's not what I was going to say."

"No," I said, without any anger. "But it's what you were thinking."

She looked away, then back at me. "Not exactly. I was just

thinking that he's used to these big money games, is all."

"The game is the game," I told her. "It doesn't matter if every chip is a dollar or a thousand dollars. The stack is the same, the player is the same, the same fifty-two cards are in the deck."

"But—"

"The game is the game," I repeated.

"Okay," she said softly. She lowered her head back to my chest.

"And I can beat him at this game," I said again.

She nodded, her hair rubbing against my bare skin. "I believe you. I know you can."

"Besides," I said, "I've been riding this luck wave for a while now."

She made a chuckling sound. "How can you say that? You lost all that money, and then what they did to your finger?"

"True," I said. "But I've been winning for the last twenty-four hours at the card tables, and before that, I met you."

She raised her eyes to mine. "Oh, Casey, that's…I…oh, Casey!" She pressed her lips to mine in a fierce, deep kiss that almost took us into another round of what got us sweaty in the first place. But then she pulled back and looked at me intensely.

"That's part of what I'm afraid of," she said.

"Afraid? Of what?"

"What happens after?"

"After the game? I pay off the Swede. You pocket some serious cash. What?"

She was shaking her head. "No, I mean with us."

I considered, then shrugged. "I don't know. I want to be with you. I don't care how we make it work."

"I can't stay here," she said. "Too much has happened. And then there's that woman, the cop…"

"Nicky," I whispered.

"Yeah. I know you said it was over, but let's be real. We're adults, and these things are never that simple. I'd be worried you'd want to go back to her. Plus, she'd be here in town, and a cop, too. Who knows what she might do to harass us?"

I shook my head. "No. It *is* over. And Nicky's not like that. She's by the book. She wouldn't bother us."

"That's why she arrested you in the casino and took you—"

"She didn't arrest me."

"*And* took you into a room like you were some kind of criminal, all because of relationship stuff? What kind of cop does that, Casey?"

"She was upset."

"That's my point. That's why I can't be here."

"So, you're leaving, then?"

"Yes."

"After the game."

"Yes."

My stomach sank. I lay still not knowing what to say, just staring back at her, trying to find the words. All I could muster was a weak, "Annie..."

"Come with me," she said.

"What?"

"Come with me. We'll leave after the game. There'll be enough money to go get started somewhere else. I don't care where. Just so we leave this dirty town, and just so we're together."

"Annie, I..."

She gave me a wounded look, as if she'd just proposed marriage and I'd asked to think it over. "Hey, no promises," she said. "If it's not working, you can bail at any time."

"I..."

She grabbed me by the shoulders. "Casey, I just want to *try*. I want to try to have something real for once in my life. Try with me. Please."

I looked into her eyes, and I didn't see someone excited to be with some ball player or looking to hitch themselves to a gravy train that was rumored to be head to the show. And she wasn't looking at me like I was some degenerate gambler who she could always feel like she was better than, or who she could save and prove her heroism, or her worth, or whatever reason Nicky had with me.

Instead, I saw someone who just saw me. Just me. And maybe for the first time in my life.

How could I say no to that?

After showering, we made our plans while I dressed in casual jeans and a button-down shirt. We'd play the game, win asshole's money, and come back here to celebrate. Tomorrow, we'd get her diamonds back, pay off the Swede, and blow town.

"Where do you want to go?"

She smiled. "Let's go south. I heard Scottsdale, Arizona is nice."

"It is," I said. "I played a season of Arizona Fall League, and they have a team there."

She draped her bra over her pert breasts, reached around, and snapped it in back. "Maybe you could get a coaching job or something?"

I shrugged. I didn't exactly leave baseball on Pete Rose terms, but it wasn't exactly a happy sendoff, either.

"Or not," she said, wriggling into her deep burgundy dress. "We'll figure it out. Hell, we can spend a couple of years figuring it out, with the kind of money we'll have." She backed toward me, pulling her hair off the back of her neck. "Will you zip me up?"

I took the zipper between my thumb and forefinger and started it upward. Then I leaned down and kissed her neck, little soft, fluttering kisses. She leaned into the kisses, reaching back with her hand to stroke my hair.

"No time, baby," she whispered. "No time now, but after… all the time in the world."

"Good," I said, pulling away and zipping her up slowly. "We'll need it, with all I've got planned."

I swatted her lightly on the ass, then squeezed.

She actually giggled, scampering across the room to her shoes. Goddamn.

"Maybe we should arrive separately," she said, slipping on her shoes.

"Why?"

"It might be better if no one knows about us. If they all just think this is a professional relationship. That you're my hired gun."

"Have gun, will travel?" I asked.

"Huh?"

"Nothing. An old TV show. I used to watch the re-runs with my Dad before he died."

"Oh."

I thought about what she said. "You're right," I decided. "If Babe doesn't know, he can't use it against me. Or tell the Swede. Either way, you're safer."

"And if Mr. Big Shot doesn't know, he can't use me against you, either," Annie added. "In fact..." she adjusted her dress slightly, accentuating her cleavage just a bit. Then she smiled. "Maybe I can distract him a little. Throw him off his game."

I gathered her into my arms. "Any man who can concentrate when you're in the room is either dead, gay, or blind."

"What about you?"

"I get a pass," I said, "because I know I'm leaving with you."

She kissed my forehead, the tip of my nose, then held a longer kiss on my lips. She squeezed my hand and let go at the same time that she broke the kiss.

"Let's ride that wave, baby," she whispered. "Let's ride it right out of town."

After she left, I waited twenty minutes. First, I sat on the edge of the bed, but that made me think of her too much, so I moved to one of the chairs instead. I sat and stared down at my hands. The bandage on my left hand was clean. I'd examined the burn in the shower, and though it was nasty looking, there didn't appear to be any infection. I wondered how long it would be before the stub of my little finger felt normal again. A year?

I took a deep breath and let it out. Another. A third. I tried to put myself back into game-day mode. Clear the entire mechanism. No Annie, no Nicky, no Babe, no Swede. Just the game in front of me. The stacks, the cards, and the son of a bitch across the table.

I kept up the slow, focused breaths. I envisioned laying down my cards and scraping pots. Dull, in the background, I imagined Annie's squeals of delight, her hands clapping. Big Shot's look of despair. Babe's look of disappointment.

The cards.

The stacks.

The son of a bitch across from me.

Bet.

Lay down the cards.

Scrape the pot.

In twenty minutes, I was more focused than I'd ever been, even when we won the Double-A championship. I was like a boxer before a fight with the champ. I could have gone on TV right then and beaten all the legends of the game and not even noticed the lights or the crowd.

I rose from the chair and walked out of the room.

Not two seconds after I walked into the lobby of the Magnum, two security guards appeared in front of me. One was Gregory. His massive form would have been enough all by itself without the side order of steroids next to him.

I half expected them to kick me out on my ass for a second, but Gregory gave me a small nod. In his quiet, unassuming voice, he said, "This way, Mr. Brunnell." Then he turned and walked across the lobby toward the elevators.

Side Order waited for me to follow, so I did.

At the elevators, we waited half a minute for the next car to arrive. The doors slid open, and we stepped inside. Gregory inserted a key into the control panel and hit a button. We were obviously going up to the executive floor.

Any other time, I might have had something wise to say, but not today. Today was game day.

The elevator dinged.

"Hold the car," Gregory told Side Order. Without waiting for an answer, he exited the elevator and led me down a short hallway. We only passed four doors before he stopped at one labeled X5 and knocked. As I looked down the hallway, I saw perhaps another ten or so doors before the turn at the corner of the building.

These weren't rooms. They were more like apartments.

I was in whale country.

The door opened, and Babe Parcella appeared in the doorway. He nodded at Gregory. Not really a thank you so much as an acknowledgment and a dismissal all in one. Then his eyes settled on me.

He smiled, shark-like.

I didn't say a word.

Neither did he. After a moment, he swung the door open to let me in.

I walked through the open entryway and into the large living room. A standard table sat in the middle of the room, chips already stacked in front of each of the two seats directly across from each other. Tala stood in the dealer's box, her hands folded in front of her, a deck of cards spread out the green felt of the table.

Annie sat on the couch nearest one of the seats. She glanced up at me and flashed a cool, confident grin.

The cowboy's manager sat next to her. He rose when I walked in, and approached. He offered me his hand, and I took it out of habit.

"Mr. Brunnell, I'm Ronnie Turnbull."

"I know."

"Yeah? Well, that's good. It's good to be known. Anyway, if you'll sit down, I'll get Cord. He's laying down in the other room."

I nodded, taking the seat nearest Annie.

A minute or two later, Cord Needham strolled out of the back bedroom, his manager on his heels. He flashed me a country-boy smile with a dose of go fuck yourself right underneath the surface and sat down. His manager hunkered down in a cushioned chair behind him.

Babe appeared at the table across from Tala next to a tall stool. Without preamble, he said, "It's heads-up play, gentlemen. Standard rules. Thousand-dollar blinds to start, doubling every twenty-one hands. No limit. I will oversee the match, any breaks, and rule on anything that needs ruling on. Afterward, the winner can see me to collect his winnings, which are in my safe down in my office. Any questions?"

I shook my head.

So did Cord.

Babe gave a nod and settled onto the high stool.

Cord and I stared at each other across the table for a few seconds. Everyone seemed to be waiting for something. Babe and Tala stood absolutely still, hardly blinking. Ronnie watched stoically from the couch near Cord. Out of the corner of my eye, I saw a flash of tanned flesh as Annie crossed her legs.

Cord noticed. He gave Annie an appreciative look, lingering there for a moment, before he turned back to me.

"Play cards," he said, like it was the tagline from some stupid movie starring him. Well, he wasn't going to like how this one ended.

Not one fucking bit.

"Let's do it," I said.

TWENTY
Cord

I have won the first five hands of this little hoop-te-doo and the dealer is flopping right now on hand number six. The money hasn't been too big yet, but winning hands is winning hands. It's early, way early, and I don't like winning everything at the beginning.

Neither one of us is too chatty, so the talk has been pretty limited. I have never played that bullshit non-stop talk game and never will. Some of the assholes in the association just never shut the hell up. Almost like it's physically impossible for them to zip it.

I'm pretty sure that he doesn't play the chat game, either. Then, of course, this ain't exactly two buddies getting together for a match, so the talk is tight.

"Call." He's charging again, but I'm staying with him. I got pocket rockets, and she just flopped another ace. A raise would've chased him off.

The perfect setup would have him holding the last bullet, thinking that he just got better. But I don't think he has shit, and I think he knows I know. Hell, Annie probably knows it. I'm gonna win the first six hands now, and things are looking good.

Speakin' of things looking good. I take a quick glance over at her. My eyes go slowly up her legs, and she does a little shift, pushing her dress up a little farther on her thigh.

She reaches and gives it a little tug down again. I keep going up and over that landscape and then come to her face. She's got a very small smile, just around the corners of those lips. Her eyes go from me, quickly to Casey, and then bang, back to me. She pulls the dress down a little further and gives me a little shift of those hips again. I go back to those green eyes and swim there for a second. I get a quick wink, too.

Well, damn.

The turn is a seven of diamonds. Casey thinks, plays with his chips, thinks some more. Keeps shuffling those chips. I think it's all drama. *C'mon boy, bet 'em up.*

"Fifty." He slides the stack of chips out there using his good hand.

Now, that bet in a tournament game is like a sneeze, a spit in the wind. In a set game like this, though, with a cap on four hundred K a piece, that's a good honest bet. The table is now ace, nine, jack, seven. River coming. Even if he's wired in the pocket, he can't beat me. He can't boat. Some kind of inside straight is a hope and a prayer. This hands over. But I want his milk on the river, too.

"I call." I'm sliding those chips to the middle without hesitation. Very deliberate. "You must have three cards in the hole."

He looks at me and then the dealer with a smartass exaggerated expression of surprise. "Wait, what? We aren't supposed to have three pocket cards?"

Then he goes back to his hole cards again and bends up the corners. Thinking, thinking and staring at the center of the table.

I pop my neck twice, bunch up my shoulders, and then let them drop. I'm smiling at him, and he's staring at me now instead of the table.

I'm overdoing it on purpose, just confident and relaxed as hell. I want him to analyze me, to start guessing. He knows that I'll be bluffing one of these hands, because I've kicked his ass with real cards so far. And he's right, I will be soon no doubt, just not this hand.

The dealer burns and turns a duck on the river. A fucking duck. Wow, that's an ugly card for whatever he was trying to do.

"Hey, Casey, been meaning to ask you...what happened to your hand, son?" I point at it and frown a little. You know, concerned.

"Check." He pats his good hand softly on the blue felt.

"Check? After all that?" I shoot my eyebrows up. He actually wants me to bet this. Now I think he's got a pair in the hole and has trips. I'm thinking he tripped on the flop with jacks maybe. Yeah, jacks. It's a beautiful thing.

"Well, hell, maybe I should just check, too." I stare at him and wait. And wait. He does nothing. Flat expression. He's good on not showing anything. Face, hands, body, and voice. Steady, methodical.

I take a drink of water, set it down.

"Eighty." I slide two stacks of chips slow and easy out into the middle of the table.

It's fish or cut bait time now for him. He rolls his eyes up slowly from the table to me.

I just stare at him. I was smiling and now I'm not, I give my mouth just a tiny little twitch. A little nonsense shit just to screw with his mind.

Another full minute clicks by and he's still staring. Slowly, a small grin appears. Then it's gone. He wanted me to see that.

"Cord, you could have gotten more money there if you would have bet that hand right." He casually tosses his cards face down into the middle of the table. "But you screwed it up. Fold."

The dealer slides the chips over to me, and I start stacking.

"Carey, you know, you're right." I keep stacking. "Wait, sorry. *Casey*, I mean. Sorry." I finally get my towers of chips just right. I straighten my WPA bracelet a little for show. "I mean, if I don't start playing better I won't be able to skunk your ass. I'll lose a hand here if I'm not careful."

"I just thought you were a little better, that's all." He takes a drink of his water, sets it down, and gives me that short, quick smile again.

The dealer is ready and off we go again.

Two cards slide my way.

I peek at a Big Slick. Clubs.

He's probably right. I went a little high on that last river bet. Could have nipped for another forty or fifty maybe. Maybe. Or he might have folded anyway.

One thing is clear though, I'm gonna beat this asshole whether I get cards or not. It's just the odds and how things go, so I'll stop getting the cards for a while. I'll slow down after coming out of the gate this quick. But I'll weather it.

I study him as he looks at his cards. Then he puts the corners down, puts his hands on the table. He looks at his chips. Grabs twenty or so thousand and plays with them. Grabs a few more and stacks them too.

Turns up the corners of cards and peeps at them again. Playing with a stack of maybe thirty thousand now, picking them up slightly and letting them fall back.

Finally, he puts ten out there. Ten.

I go back to my cards. Lots of hearts have been broken with the ol' Big Slick. It looks damn good, but you gotta be careful with it. They're just cards, but it's funny how some hands rarely go right for you.

Then again, I won a tournament in London two years ago with the Big Slick. I think it was pups, too. No straight or anything. Paired a king on the turn if I remember right. Took the pot *and* the tournament with that hand.

Like I said, they're just cards. You just can't play with that "always a lucky hand, always a bad hand" bullshit floating around in your head. I'm gonna push him now and keep on pushing. Hard.

"Forty, to see the flop." I push his ten and thirty more out there.

"See it." An immediate response, but calm. No expression from him. Pops those chips right out there. I mean, what's he gonna do, right? He could have folded, but he'd lose the blind. After losing the first five hands, ol' Casey over there needs a win. His baby needs new shoes. Now.

I drain my drink and hold it up to a guy over in the corner of the room at a small wet bar. I didn't even see him when I walked in. He looks like part of the furniture. Three pops is my own personal limit in a private game and none of course at a tournament final table. I could play on five or six and still win, but I stay a helluva lot sharper this way.

Ronnie gets up from the couch, gets my tumbler, and walks over to the wet bar. He holds up two fingers to the guy.

The dealer deals. Burns and turns. I'll be damned if she doesn't turn a queen of spades, jack of hearts, and then ever so slowly the third card. A six. It's a shitty little six of diamonds.

Nothing on the flop suits up with me, so I'm looking for a lady all the way now. I could pair up a cowboy or bullet maybe, but I doubt it.

I've been staring at him on the flop, watching his eyes, mostly hoping to get something there, because like I said he don't show me shit otherwise. He's very good at that. Better than most pros I've played.

"Twenty."

He bet quick again, changing his pace with this hand. I think about that ten-grand opening bet now. It seems, or he's acting like it anyway, he's got this fuckin' hand. Knows exactly how it's gonna roll. Seems that way.

Ronnie brings my drink over, then walks back to the couch with his but doesn't sit right away.

I should be thinking about my bet, and I am, but that doesn't mean I can't do a little window shopping. I give Annie a quick glance, and we hook up with our eyes again. She crosses those legs again, and I look away.

"Twenty and another twenty."

He gives me a casual glance as he put another twenty out there.

The turn is coming now.

Ronnie sits down again.

Parcella crosses his arms and moves from side to side a little.

Annie bends forward slightly and then sits back again.

Ten. Ten of hearts.

I purse my lips and nod my head slightly, which I do all the time, good hand or bad hand.

If he has a straight on the low end, I've got him. No flushes out there. I suppose he could draw into a boat or an ace-high straight like mine on the river card. I don't see that, though, and don't feel it either.

"Check," he says.

"Not this again?"

He looks at me with a bland, bored look.

"All in," I say.

He doesn't hesitate. "Take it."

Not sure, but I think he threw away a small straight—just couldn't risk it this early.

Seven hands in a row. I haven't been this hot coming right out of the gates for a long time. He's also getting short stacked. Those last two big hands really hurt him. We're not even at two hours of play yet. This game can turn at any time, though. Just gotta keep playing the cards.

"Mr. Parcella, how about a short break? I don't know, fifteen minutes maybe?" Pretty obvious that Casey is just trying to put the brakes on at this point. Stop the momentum somehow.

Parcella slides off the stool slowly and looks over at me. "Cord? It's early yet, but do you have a problem with that?"

"Not a problem." I stand up and give a couple of twists at the waist. "Uncle Mo will wait for me."

"All right then, how about twenty minutes? The suites on this level all have balconies as well if you want some air."

Casey gets up, too. Leans over to Annie and says something. Across the room, Ronnie leaves the couch a little stiff-legged. Annie stays seated.

"Everyone, I forgot to mention that there are snacks at the wet bar, but I can have something ordered up too. Just let me know. Restrooms directly across the hall from us."

He immediately gets on his cell phone and slowly walks to another corner of the big room.

I walk over to Annie, and I can feel Casey's eyes following me from across the room. He's over by the wet bar looking at what snacks they had.

"Hello, Ms. Kozak."

"Mr. Needham." She nods, eyes all ablaze, just looking up at me. I swear, whatever that perfume is that she wears, I'm gonna buy her a boatload so she never runs out.

"Could I drink you a buy…I mean, can I buy you a drink?"

She grins and gets up out of her chair.

"I stole that line from a country song. George Strait."

"You know, I think I will. Just a Chardonnay or whatever white wine they have."

I walk over to the wet bar, and Casey is just coming away from it. He has a can of Coke, a bag of cashews, and a Hershey bar.

"The breakfast of champions." I decide to keep it light.

"Yep." He pauses instead of walking away.

I look from him to the bartender.

"I'll take a glass of Chardonnay and an ice water."

"Did Annie order that?"

"Yessir."

The bartender pours a generous amount into a stemmed glass.

"I already asked her on the break. Here, I'll take it to her."

"Uh, no, you won't. What did she say when you asked her?"

Casey's jaw starts working, but he doesn't answer.

"Well, there you go, ace. What's that tell you, Lover Boy?"

He laughs then, and I didn't expect that.

We stare at each other for a moment more. Out of the corner of my eye, I can see Ronnie watching us, even though he's talking to Babe Parcella about something.

"I'm gonna love taking your money and kicking your ass," he

says, his voice dropping a little lower.

"Wake me up when that starts, okay? Seriously."

"Starts right now...Seriously."

He walks away, but when he looks back over his shoulder, I sure don't like that grin or the look in his eye.

TWENTY-ONE
Casey

The break was more like thirty minutes before we made it back to the table. I slammed a candy bar and chased it with Coke, hit the bathroom quick, and came back to find Cord chatting up Annie.

Even though I knew it was part of the plan, even though I *knew* she was acting, just stringing him along to throw him off his game, it bothered me. The low cut of her dress and how his eyes drifted to her chest. How close he stood to her. The intimate little laugh he had with her as I was walking in. The way she touched his forearm lightly, then pulled it away when she heard the door close.

She was good at this. Very good. And it bothered me.

I couldn't let it throw me off my game, though. Between getting some shitty cards on a few hands and folding a winner on a couple others, I'd managed to bolster his confidence. Not that the arrogant prick needed much in the way of self-confidence, but this was cards. If someone gets used to winning, they think they'll continue to win. They don't pay attention to the odds or the outside chances. And that's the ones that hurt the most. The bad beats you don't see coming.

With all the eye-fucking he's been giving Annie, and winning seven straight to open this shindig, I figured he had to be swimming in self-confidence now.

It was time to find out.

"Let's play cards, y'all," I twanged.

Cord acted like he'd barely heard me. He finished his sentence with Annie, gave her an "aw shucks" chuckle, and strolled back to the table.

I cracked open a bottle of mineral water and took a sip. Then I popped a couple of cashews in my mouth and chewed. I could feel the sugar rush coming, and the timing couldn't be better.

He sat down across from me, and Babe took up his position of oversight, crossing his burly arms and putting on a neutral expression. I glanced at him, and I swear I could see a slight smirk under his so-called professionalism. I knew if I won, he'd call the Swede at the first opportunity he had. Hell, that was probably the phone call he made during the break.

It didn't matter. The game mattered.

He slid in the blind.

"At this rate," he said, "we won't need to bump these blinds. No way this is going twenty-one hands." He gave me that tight, fake casual smile meant to rattle me.

Keep talking, asshole, I thought.

"We'll see," was all I said.

Tala finished shuffling and dealt. I waited to look at my cards and watched Cord instead. I knew I was blanking him when it came to tells, but he was no easy read, either. His reactions seemed to be the same whether the cards were strong or weak. All the pros and all the manuals say that you play the man more than the cards or the stacks, but when the man refuses to give you anything, all you can do is make sure you give the same or less in return and play the cards.

Cord looked at his cards. Showed me nothing. No micro-tells, no tightening or relaxing around the mouth or eyes. No glances that meant anything, as far as I could tell.

Then he looked at me. After a moment, he smiled again and purposefully turned his gaze to Annie. Gave her an appreciative stare.

I let it be. He wasn't going to get to me. After this game was over, after I kicked his ass and took his money, that woman was leaving with me. She would be warming my bed, and this cowboy, his manager, fucking Babe and the Swede and even Nicky could all kiss my ass goodbye. I was moving on to better things.

Cord brought his gaze back to me. Without looking away, he slid two short stacks out. "Let's see the blind, plus twenty-five."

He was pushing hard. My stacks were down under three hundred, probably closer to two-twenty or two-forty. He figured to bully his way through the second half of my chips. Buy as many pots as he could.

"Call," I said.

His eyebrows went up. "Blind call now? Son, you must be desperate."

I gave him a flat stare. "You'll have to pay to find out."

He chuckled. "Mister, I don't pay for anything unless I decide I *want* to pay for it. So don't go thinking you're going to push me into something reckless."

"Don't go thinking you're going buy your way through the rest of my stack," I replied.

He just chuckled a little more, shaking his head and casting a flirtatious look at Annie.

I waited for Tala to flop. She laid out a four, a ten, and a jack, not a one of them in the same suit. I peeked at my own cards. A pair of jacksons. Throw in the one on the table, and I was looking at My Three Sons.

Trips was strong enough to win, and I still had two cards to build on. Maybe get the fourth prince or swing a full boat.

Of course, with two cards left, he could steal the hand, too.

I waited.

He pursed his lips and nodded at the flop, just like he had all seven hands previous. Then he pushed three stacks out.

"Thirty."

"Call," I said without hesitation.

I could feel this one building. There are a few hands in every tournament that the entire game turns on. Two, really. The one that sets the path, and the one that ends the game. It was too early for this one to end yet, but this one felt big. Like it would be the one to set the path, and all the other hands would just be playing out the inevitable.

Tala burned and turned. A three. No help for either of us. He could be working a low end straight, but I doubted it. No way would he have bet that aggressively when the most he could've had at the outset was three of the five cards he needed. That was loser play, something guys did after six beers at their weekly game at their buddy's house. Of course, those bastards actually hit their card on the river and pissed off all their friends, but that was blue-collar, fifty-cent and quarter games.

Not here.

"Another thirty," Cord said, pushing the stacks out.

I paused. Could he be building around a top end straight? He could have four of the five cards now, if he was holding a nine and a lady. Or a royal couple.

But damn, he was betting strong for someone still looking for love at the river.

I made my decision. "See your thirty," I said, "and twenty more."

He grinned. "We gonna compare cocks now, huh?" He looked over at Annie. "Beggin' your pardon, ma'am."

Annie shrugged.

Cord turned back to me. "All right, ace. It's your show. Call."

We waited. Tala burned the top card, then hesitated, just slightly, with that built-in sense of drama that all good dealers get when they're about to turn an important card.

She flipped the card.

Ace of hearts.

Cord pursed his lips and nodded. "Let's go another fifty, stud."

I waited for him to push his chips into the center. The stack was already big enough to draw me just about back to even. Or, if I lost, pretty much end the game except for the formality of playing out the hands.

"Okay, big spender," I said. I pushed out fifty and chased it with another fifty. "Double it."

Cord paused, a sly smile playing on his lips. I knew that there were cards he could have in his hand that had me beat. Hell, if he was holding that royal couple I mentioned, he was sitting on an ace-high straight right now. And with no pair on the table, he knew I couldn't be holding a full boat or a foursome, so that narrowed down the possibilities. A flush wasn't possible, either. Which meant that if he held that straight, he knew he couldn't be beat.

If I were in his shoes, I'd go all in. It was the only real play. And if he did, with all those rounders on the table, I'd have to call. Too much to lose, even if he had the straight. In for a penny, in for a pound.

He slid fifty thousand into the center. "See that," he said, "and raise ten more." He pushed the small stack in behind the large one.

Ten?

Fucking *ten*?

He had me confused for a second. If he had the straight, he knew he couldn't lose. All-in buys the pot if it forces me to fold or it wins the game outright if I call. But he only bets *ten*? What the hell was that?

I stared at him, but he showed me nothing. Just that smart-alec confident grin playing on his lips like a shitty country song. I looked at the massive pile of chips in the center of the table. I didn't dare count how much was in there, but a win would have to put me slightly ahead of him.

And a loss would be damn near mortal.

But *ten*?

I looked at the cards again. He couldn't have the ace-high straight. Not with that bet. So what the hell was this cowboy holding?

Did he have bullets under there?

Or two bits? A two and a five under gave him a low end straight. But Jesus, there was no way in hell he would have bet so strong at the flop with just three cards out of a straight. And not even open-ended. And the bet before the river, still not holding shit?

Was he trying to bluff me and maybe backed into this straight?

Three possibilities. He either had a pair of aces or a two and a five, or I'd win this monster pot.

"Call," I said, before I was even aware I was going to say it, and I pushed ten thousand into the center of the table. "Now show."

"I know the rules, son," Cord said, his easy smile not making it to his eyes when he looked at me. There was some definite dislike there, and maybe some disgust, too, but I saw one other thing along the first two.

Doubt.

Just a flicker of doubt.

He reached out and turned his cards over with an expert flick of the wrist.

Tens.

Plus the one on the table. Trips tens.

Cord's smile broadened. "That's thirty miles of bad road, friend."

I smiled back, masking my relief. I wanted him to think I'd known the outcome all along. Set him up for that bluff that I'd have to pull at some point, just like he'd be trying to do the same to me.

I turned over my jacks and watched his eyes.

His smile faded slightly, but then he pursed his lips and nodded. "Well played," he said quietly.

I scraped the pot and stacked my chips. No one said a word. When I looked across at his stacks, they looked smaller than the ones in front of me.

"Play cards," I said, just as quietly.

QUEEN OF DIAMONDS

The hands went fast after that, and play was ragged. We both let blinds go, based on shitty hole cards, and we each took a few small pots. Neither of us made any aggressive moves. No one said anything. There was just the sound of the cards on the felt, the clink of chips, and a few muted words to make bets.

We were like two fighters, having landed a couple of big bombs early, who prowl around the ring carefully, feinting and jabbing and trying to figure out how to land that big shot again without getting hammered by the other guy first.

His manager had a nervous expression that he was trying to hide. I don't think he expected someone like me, who he figured for a rabbit, to give his boy any kind of a run.

Babe stood, his expression impassive, watching.

I dared not give Annie a look, knowing what that would do to my concentration. I noticed Cord had slacked off on the looks he was casting her way, too.

We doubled the blinds and played on. The biggest hand I took was about sixty, and the biggest I lost was around forty, but I lost a couple of those. More and more, we were both giving up on the blinds if the dealt cards didn't have any play. It was conservative poker, and it was the kind of gameplay that made for a long night.

We took another break after a few hours. I used the restroom, washed my hands, and splashed cold water on my face. I stared down at my bandaged finger. Over the past day, I'd almost become accustomed to the dull throb that came with every heartbeat. Extra Strength Tylenol kept it from being excruciating. I wished for some perks or hydros or something, but it would have to wait until after the game. I had to stay sharp.

I ran my good hand through my hair, letting the water slick it back a little. The wet look had been out since the eighties, but the water on my face and in my hair made me feel fresh. And who knew how long this was going to go on.

When I exited the bathroom, I almost bumped into Annie.

Her mouth found mine before I could say a word. Her kiss was desperate and deep. When she broke it off, I was unable to speak for a moment.

"You have to push him," she whispered. "He's biding his time until the time is right. Don't let him decide when. *You* decide."

"I thought you didn't know this game well enough to play him," I said. "I thought—"

"I know people," she answered me, glancing over her shoulder to see if anyone was coming into the suite on this side. "And I can tell what he's up to. It's obvious."

"I'm playing him even," I said. "I'm just as good as he is."

"Be better." She kissed me again, this time more softly. Then she asked me, "That wave you always talk about? Are you riding it, Casey?"

I looked into her green eyes, and I saw the rest of my life there. It didn't get any luckier than that.

"I am."

"Then finish it," she said.

She brushed past me and went into the bathroom. Her perfume wafted in the air, remaining there in her wake after she left. I breathed it in, that soft, subtle, powerful scent. I could still taste her on my lips.

"I will," I said after her, even though I knew she couldn't hear me from behind the door.

I walked through the small suite and into the huge main room. Babe stood in his usual spot, his arms crossed like he didn't know any other pose. Cord's manager sat on the couch behind him, nursing some amber liquid, looking nervous. Tala stood, the cards fanned out in front of her, with an expression to match Babe's.

And Cord. He was already seated at the table, leaning back in his chair and watching me.

I strode to the table and sat down.

"The little lady?" Cord asked.

I shrugged. "Bathroom."
"You wanna wait for her?"
I shook my head. "Play cards," I said.
Cord nodded, not smiling. "Oh, yeah."

TWENTY-TWO
Cord

It's about 4:15 a.m. now. We've been going back and forth and back again. Winning some, losing some. Slowly, though, I lost my chip lead. A big hand he won right before we broke had really hurt. It wasn't about just losing the chip lead at this point. It was about losing.

"You all right?" Ronnie asks me.

"Of course, I'm all right. Tired and all, but then again, we're not exactly digging ditches here. I think I'll survive."

"It's getting time to end it, Cord. The longer this goes, the more I don't like it."

"Now there, there is a couple of news flashes. You think I still want to be playing? I've been up past my bedtime before, though. I've played better card players, too...and won."

Ronnie leans in closer. "The third to last hand before this break? Never saw the inside straight. The bastard played it well. Bet it well." He takes a sip and looks away. "Cord, he's getting the cards, and he knows how to play them."

"He's getting my money, too. We were just trading off for a long time, but he's gonna try to roll me over now. I got him, though. I got him."

"Win or lose, you worried about her after this? With him and all?"

"No, the prick signed the paper saying they were all square.

The paper means nothing, of course, but it does publicly tie him to her with a bunch of witnesses. He'd be a fool to try and hurt her now."

Ronnie gives me a doubtful look.

"Hey, this is what he really wanted." I point at my chest. "*I'm* what he really wanted. Fucker hates me for some reason. He wants the win and to get the money, sure. But he wants to rub my nose in it, too. Besides, fuck it. All three of us are leaving here for A.C. as soon as this is over. You bought that third ticket, right?"

"Yep. Don't like it, but yeah, I did."

"All right then. Well, like you said, time to get this thing over with. I'm gonna break his heart."

"Need anything before I go over to the couch and pass out?"

I hold up my empty tumbler to him. "I could use one more of these."

Ronnie just grinned at me.

"Bad idea, Cord. You've already gone over your limit for this kind of little show."

"Yeah, I know, just saying."

"I'll get you a bottle of water."

We had just finished eating a little something from two impressive food trays that had been brought up about twenty minutes ago.

Parcella had acted like it was all for us, but by the way he wolfed down two of those giant roast beef sandwiches, it was pretty obvious he had been starving.

Ronnie and I split up now as we get closer to the table. We had all agreed on just a quick fifteen-minute break. Casey is already seated at the table, and Annie is in her chair off to the side, looking at the table and sipping a Coke.

I try to catch her eye, but she was staring a hole through the towers of chips in front of Casey.

I could tell she was counting. She was probably worried about me getting too far down. Her smooth, tan legs crossed, uncrossed and then they crossed again. Definitely some nerves going on there.

"Mr. Needham, Mr. Brunnell, are we about ready to go here?" Babe smiles that car-salesman smile of his, claps his hands softly, and looks over at Tala. She is already seated and patiently waiting.

Despite the grin, it's clear to me that Babe would rather be at the dentist right now having his wisdom teeth pulled. I'm sure he had thought this thing would be a quick knockout.

"Yessir," I say, pulling my chair out slowly and nodding to Casey, who gives me a snotty little chin nod back.

I do catch Annie's look this time, and she flashes a quick, weak grin. One of those "I think I'm gonna puke" smiles. Can't say as I blame her. She's not used to watching people win or lose four hundred grand, and right now, he's got more than two-thirds of the chips.

"Good to go here, too." Casey's voice is calm and even. He looks up at Parcella and then slides his gaze back over to me.

Nine times out of ten, I'd beat this nobody shithead, and this will be one of those nine times. I gotta move on him before he moves on me, though, because I can't afford it otherwise.

"Great. Tala, the table is ready."

Tala deals the down cards, and we both take a peek.

I'm looking at nothing. Jack of spades. Trey, diamonds. Not suited up, can't stretch, nothing.

I short stack a bet in front of me and pause, riffling them up and down. I stop, start again, stop. Then, with my other hand, I get another short stack counted out. Twenty more. I leave them there though and just play with them, hovering over the extra twenty.

I look at him as if I'm searching him. I bring the extra twenty back into my main stacks and just slide the original twenty out in the middle for my bet.

He stares at me. I stare back. It's useless for each of us, because he don't show shit and I sure as hell don't. It's habit though. You play your game. So, we stare some more.

There hasn't even been a flop yet, but we both know what's up here. Bets and bullshit are going to come fast now. Him looking to take me out, and me looking to stop the bleeding by trying to take control of the pace.

He's thinking that little drama just now on the opening bet was a bunch of shit, or that I *wanted* him to think that was a bunch of shit.

He just sees my opening bet and the flop is more nothing. Queen, four, nine. Club, heart and heart.

I throw a thirty thousand dollar bet immediately.

He sees the bet almost as quick.

Just as quick, I glance at Babe of all people. I haven't done that all night, and I'm hoping Casey didn't miss it.

Parcella looks at me like "what the fuck?"

I could have waited, but I just can't wait on this hand anymore.

"All in." I look down and give the green table just the smallest of grins. Purposely, I don't look at Casey right away, then I do, but I don't stare.

Casey doesn't say anything. He's boring into me with his hands together under his chin.

I look at him, then flick my look to the pot, then back to him.

He knows I don't signal like this. He also knows I got nothing, *knows* it. He doesn't have anything either, though. At least, I don't think so. Plus, I'm playing the nervous thing hard to him, maybe a little too hard. Maybe I do have it, and I'm playing him that way. He'll just wait for better things, he can afford to.

Sure as hell, his two cards go to the middle, face down. "Have it, stud."

I don't say anything but give him a very small shake of my head back and forth just for the hell of it. Could be I'm disappointed in how I underplayed such a strong hand.

Hey, it was an average pot, but not to me. Coming right after the break was big. I need every chip I can find. I'm gonna beat this fucker to the punch on every hand. Control it, control him.

There are players who are good enough to be on the tour, make final tables, and win a tournament, but they aren't and don't. Reason is, they can't finish.

I look over at him as Tala is dealing two cards down, and he's just calmly stacking and restacking those chips. He's thinking, though.

Casey is one of those guys that is definitely "good enough." Trouble is it takes more than that. They get a chip lead, sometimes a big one like this, and then they make camp. They sit and try to have the game come to them, to win it sooner or later. I know I have him.

And as it turns out, I do have him.

"All in." It's the third time I've done this since winning that first hand off the break with a jack, trey in my hand. My watch says a little before six a.m.

Second time after that, I didn't have anything either. Casey stayed, and it was over if he had anything, but I won it with a Cowboy high if you can believe that.

This time, though, Tala just flopped me right into a beautiful hidden straight. We bet the flop, then the turn card was nothing. A diamond deuce.

I'm holding the jack of clubs, ten of hearts. She has laid out a queen of hearts, nine and eight of diamonds. Enough gap showing so that there's no alarm bells. Oh Tala, I think I love you.

Casey looks at my stacks, does a quick count and then says, "Babe, what's his chip count, just for sure?"

I sit back from the table so there is no obstruction. Casey is staring at me as the chips are confirmed. I stare back, then at his coin stacks and back to him again.

"If you stay with him and you win the hand, you win the game. If you stay and lose, you have roughly a thousand dollars left and you're dead." When Parcella said "you're dead" to Casey, I could have sworn he had a twinkle in his eye.

Something very spooky about Babe Parcella.

"Hey, that's the way I had it figured too. Hell of a deal, huh?" I look at Casey all wide-eyed and shocked. Overdoing the smartass bit big time.

I was trying to send him the old "please don't stay" bullshit. If he stays, I have him and this thing is over. He's thinking I got nothing. I know it.

Ronnie gets up off the couch stiffly and walks over a little closer.

I see Annie stand from her chair too, straightening her dress and pulling it down a little. She looks at me, but she's so nervous she can't even smile. Her face is flat, with no expression, tight and drawn. The green eyes are drop dead gorgeous as always, but they don't talk to me this time.

"Oh, I'm definitely in, Cord." He flipped his cards on the table showing a harmless four of clubs but a seven of diamonds, too. "I mean, with a flush hand just waiting to happen, she's screaming at me to stay. How can I fold, right?" He shoots me a tight smile that just stones me.

He knows he's going to win. He can feel it. And you know what? I do, too. Right then. In that moment.

I give Annie a fake smile to help boost her spirits a little. Finally, a small smile comes back from her. Trouble is, I think it was more fake than mine.

"Well, you do what you gotta do. I'll just play these the way they are." I throw my jack and ten out showing the straight.

Tala scans the table quickly and begins. She burns a card and then brings the still turned-down river card out into the middle of the table.

"Who's she, by the way?"

"What?" Casey says quickly with his eyebrows scrunched together. His eyes don't leave Tala's delicate fingers.

Tala gives it the dramatic pause. Even she seems to want to

know.

"Who's the bitch screaming at you?"

He looks at me then. "Cord, any diamond will do it. But she? She's the queen of diamonds."

He glances back at Annie and smiles. "The queen of diamonds is coming up."

And as he says it, Tala turns over that exact card.

TWENTY-THREE
Casey

There are moments in your life that you wish would last forever. Three, maybe four of them in a lifetime, if you're lucky.

When I called for the queen of diamonds, I knew that one of those moments was about to happen. I was flush with power, luck, energy, whatever you want to call it. I didn't calculate the odds that she was the next card. No thoughts about how it was one in fifty-two. That's minus his, minus the burns, one of which could've been my queen, and minus the table cards. Odds didn't matter, because I was riding the wave, and...I...*knew*.

Everyone froze when Tala turned over my queen. No one sullied that beautiful moment with a sharp intake of breath, or a groan, or a muttered "shit." They all just froze in that moment, and like I said, I wished it had lasted forever.

After the long, stunned silence passed and the moment was gone, I heard Cord's manager sigh and mumble something I couldn't hear. Cord didn't say a word, though. Not right away. He looked long and hard at that queen, then finally up to me.

I stared back at him.

Slowly, he stood and walked around the table toward me. I wasn't sure what he was going to do, so I pushed myself back from the table so I could rise or get away if he decided to get rough. I shouldn't have been worried, though.

He stuck out his hand. "Good game, pardner," he said. I

heard some disappointment in his voice, but maybe some grudging respect, too. Or maybe I just imagined that part.

I shook his hand. "Thanks," I said.

He motioned to the bar. "After that, I think we need a drink. Whaddaya say?"

I glanced over at Annie. She gave me a subtle nod, so I shrugged. "Sure, why not?"

Cord smiled and walked to the wet bar.

"Maker's all right with you?"

"Yeah." At that point, anything was all right with me. I stared down at all the chips on the table. Eight hundred thousand dollars. All mine and Annie's. Even after I paid off the Swede, and she got her diamonds back, there was still a fortune left. We could leave Vegas, go wherever. We could—

"I thought I had you," Cord said, clinking the bottle onto the lip of the glass while he poured.

"When?"

"About three times," he said.

"Which?"

Cord chuckled, his back still to me. "Nah, if I told you that, you'd be able to beat me again. And believe me, son, *that* isn't going to happen."

A cold shot went through me. For a second, I thought he was going to welsh on the deal. It was just him and the manager, but if Babe were in on it, too, that'd leave me and Annie to go up against the three of them. Hardly a fair fight, especially with my fucked-up finger.

But before the fear subsided and I could even start to get pissed, Cord turned around with a glass in each hand. "I expect there'll be another game somewhere down the road," he said. "I mean, you're good enough to play in my circles, so no doubt we'll end up at the same table again."

He put the glass on the table in front of me. I picked it up. "No doubt," I said.

He nodded. "There ya go." He held out his glass, and I clinked it soundly.

We drank.

The whiskey was harsh, but the heat of it felt good on my scratchy throat. I took another sip, swallowed, and nodded. "Good stuff."

"Some of the best, at least in my book," Cord said. He turned and walked back to his chair. "Ronnie, you wanna give two card players a few minutes?" He looked at everyone else in the room. "Y'all mind, too?"

Tala was the first to turn to go. I stopped her, sliding a stack of five thousand across the table in her direction. She smiled and nodded her thanks. I thought about it another half second and slid a second stack. Her smile broadened, and she reached for the chips, saying, "Thank you."

I looked up at Babe and made sure he saw the exchange.

He waved dismissively. "Leave the chips, Tala. I saw. Ten large."

Tala set her stacks back on the table.

"Come on down with me," Babe said to her, "and I'll cash you out." He looked back to me. "You, too, Casey. My office."

"I'll be there in a few," I said. I had to admit, I was savoring this moment, too. It was nothing like seeing that diamond-clad lady turn up on the felt, but it still felt good. I was beyond his grasp now, and he knew it. I just became a whale, and if it wasn't for the fact that I was leaving this shithole town, I'd be rubbing his nose in it for the long time to come.

Annie rose and drifted toward the door. I caught her eye. She made a small gesture with her hand, emulating a wave.

I smiled. I couldn't help it.

All three of them left, followed by Cord's manager. Then it was just the two of us. We looked at each other across the table for a few seconds, but the intensity wasn't as sharp as during the game. His friendly demeanor didn't seem as forced, either. I didn't think he was showing me everything, but he definitely wasn't playing cards any longer, either.

"What did that mean?" He motioned toward the door with his drink and raised his eyebrows.

"What did what mean?"

He smiled and took another drink, waiting.

I didn't answer.

The silence hung there for a while. Cord took another drink, then said, "Friend, I come from a part of the country where folks speak their mind plainly. So, you reckon we can have that kind of a conversation here? Seeing as how all the chips are yours now?"

I nodded. "Yeah, we can talk."

"Then don't bullshit me. You know what I meant."

"Annie?"

He lifted his glass to me. "Now we're talking."

I shrugged. "It's an inside joke."

"Tell me."

"Well, not a joke, actually. Just an inside thing."

He sipped again, thinking about that. Then he said, "So you and the lady there, you've got a thing?"

It was my turn to shrug. "You didn't know?"

He gave his head a small shake. "Can't say as I did. Leastways, not that sort of thing."

"She was my second."

"Oh, I knew *that*. And I knew—or I *thought* I knew—a few other things, too. Only now I'm not so sure."

"What're you talking about?"

"First, tell me what that little hand gesture meant. That inside thing of yours." He smiled, but there was no humor in it.

"She meant it to be a wave," I said.

"As in riding a wave?"

"Yeah."

"As in luck?"

"Exactly."

He nodded slowly. "Sometimes luck wins out," he said, pointing to the table. "Today's a good example of that. But over time?" He stopped nodding and gave his head a small shake. "Luck only carries a man so far. Skill is the lion's share."

"You saying I don't have skill?" I asked, bristling. "Because I just kicked your ass, in case you weren't paying attention."

Cord smiled indulgently. "Oh, I was paying close attention, friend. I paid attention to the cards and to your stacks and to you. I can still feel the burn of that last card, too. But I paid attention to a little more than that."

I was getting tired of this conversation. "Good for you," I said, draining my drink and standing up. "Maybe you'll learn something."

I turned to leave.

"You're in it together, aren't you?" he asked.

I froze, and that was all the answer he needed.

"I figured," he said. He let out a short sigh and drained his own glass. "Just wish I'd figured it sooner."

I narrowed my eyes. "What the hell are you talking about?"

He pointed at my empty glass. "You want another rip, ace? Because I think you're gonna need it."

I shook my head, confused.

"No? Well, I'm going to. After all, I just lost almost half a mill." He rose and went to the wet bar.

"What the hell are you talking about?" I repeated to his back.

The bottle clinked on the glass as he poured. "Let me tell you a story, son. Goes like this. A smoking hot blonde girl with a killer bod and eyes like green fire says to a guy, can you help me? I'm in trouble, she says. He's going to hurt me unless I pay him."

A cold tickle crept up my spine.

Cord set the bottle down and turned around. "But, she says, he'll let me off if only you just play cards with him. Will you save me, she asks. Will you be my hero?" He smiled tightly and takes a drink.

"No," I said, my mind scrambling to keep up. She must've been playing him, that's all. Playing him to set him up for the game.

"Yes," Cord answered. "She sucked me right in, too."

It was all part of the game, I told myself. She didn't tell me about working him, but it didn't matter. It was just a play she made to make sure I got to the table, so I could beat him. Because she knew I could.

"Tough to say no, though," Cord continued, "the way she comes at you, so ferocious."

I clenched my jaw and stood up. "Fuck you," I said.

Cord nodded. "Yessir, she did. More than once. And you, too, I'm guessin'. And I wonder if she's not fucking the both of us again, right now as we speak."

I wanted to charge at him and punch the shit out of him. Finish what I started down on the casino floor a few days ago. Knock that smug look off his face.

Cord stared back at me, calm.

"You're just pissed that I beat you," I said.

"That I am," he admitted. "But it'll pass. Everyone gets beat sometimes." He shook his head. "She played me, friend. And she's probably playing you, too."

"No way. You're only saying that because she chose me over you. Maybe she conned you, but—"

"She did more than con me," Cord interrupted. "She set me up. She distracted me with her body and her smell and every other goddamned hot thing about her. Even during the game, she was flashing me the inside of her thigh."

"I beat you fair and square."

"I'm not saying you didn't. I'm sayin' she set me up. I can see it now, and I feel the fool for it, but that don't change nothing." He took another drink and looked at me over the rim of his glass.

I shook my head. "I don't believe it. You're a sore loser. Go fuck yourself."

He didn't say another word, just kept draining his glass.

I didn't wait for him to finish. I turned around and strode out of the room, slamming the door behind me.

Arrogant son of a bitch.

Thinks he can't lose to me legit?

I walked down the short hall toward the elevator, clenching and unclenching my fists. My finger pinged in pain every time I did it, but I couldn't stop. Small doubts had crept into my mind. Why'd she play him that way?

I punched the call button and waited, shifting from foot to foot.

Why didn't she tell me?

The elevator dinged, and the doors opened. I got on board and hit the lobby button.

It didn't matter, I decided. She had her reasons, and it didn't matter. Maybe she wanted to keep me focused. Maybe she worried that I might be distracted too, only with jealousy.

"Maybe he's full of shit," I said out loud, and my own voice had a reassuring sound to it.

Yeah. The cowboy was full of shit.

The elevator car zipped downward, giving me a feeling of lightness.

I decided that in the end, it didn't matter. She chose me because I was a winner. And I proved it back in that suite, beating one of the best poker players in the world today. All that was left was for me to go down to Babe's office and collect my money. Meet her and blow this town for good. I could ask her a thousand questions once we were away and safe. And she could explain it all to me.

The elevator lurched to a stop and the door slid open. Mats the Rat stood there, smiling.

"Hello, Casey," he said. "You lucky fuck."

TWENTY-FOUR
Cord

About a minute after Lover Boy leaves, Ronnie comes back into the suite and slides behind the little bar I'm parked in front of. He quickly gurgles out a drink from the bottle of Maker's.

I tilt my hat back and stare at my boots.

"So, it's true, then. What happens in Vegas, stays in Vegas?" His voice is quiet and sarcastic.

I turn to look back at the deserted green card table with the bright Magnum logo painted in the middle, cards and stacks of chips. What catches my eye though is only one card.

I'll be thinking about that queen of diamonds for a long, long time.

"Yeah, it stays here all right. I lost a tournament, got threatened with some dredged up shit from the past and lost a money challenge to some local monkey. Hell, I can't even ride away with the girl at the end."

My turn to pour a drink, and I don't cheat myself. This could turn into a very ugly night.

I lift slowly and sip.

"I saw our boy just now from the other end of the hallway." Ronnie nods toward the door. "He was storming toward the elevators with steam comin' out his fuckin' ears. What in blue hammered hell has he got to be pissed about?"

"Cancel that third ticket on our flight, okay?"

He nods slowly at me, and his mouth becomes a tight thin line. "I tried to tell you about that little—"

"Don't!" I point a quick finger at him, and my voice is a little too strong, a little too loud.

"I'm just sayin'."

"Well, don't. Don't you *even* fuckin' say...anything." I take another sip and glare at him. It's Ronnie, though, and I look away.

He doesn't say anything more, just stares straight ahead at nothing.

The guy I trust more than anyone else in this world, more than myself, didn't deserve that just now. This sure as hell ain't his fault. He was right, he tried to tell me.

There is a long and very loud silence in the room.

I drink. He drinks.

I clear my throat finally and change the elbow I'm leaning on.

"There any smokes back behind there, pard?" I ask quietly.

We both know the code behind the tone of my voice. That tone says, I'm sorry bud, I'm an idiot and you were right.

"You don't smoke anymore, Cord." He looks at me, at least.

"There any smokes back behind there, pard?" I give him a half smile, raise my eyebrows.

"Yes, but they're not your brand. Unless you've switched to Virginia Slims, girly boy." He meets my eye, shaking his head back and forth slowly. "Now, asshole, can we talk about all of this shit, please?"

"What's to talk about? It's all laid out right on that table over there."

"Money is money, Cord."

"That was deep." I smile at him and take a sip.

"We win and lose money for a living. You and I both know the money will always come and go."

"Yeah, well, it's been goin' more than comin' lately." I can feel the liquor sneaking up on me a little. Playing cards for the last umpteen hours might have a little to do with it, too. I'm just tired. Really tired.

"So, she was doing him, too, then?"

He is so good at that. Ronnie was able to easy go it with you and then just bang, cold cock you with a question like that.

It stung, but it needed to be said.

"Yep." It's my turn to stare straight ahead.

"Screwing around with you boys is one thing, and how she'll probably try to screw him out of that money is another, but we're missing something here."

I pick up the bottle of Maker's Mark and smile over at him. "What we're missing is about half a bottle of this already. Another pop?"

"Sure, why the hell not?"

I cap my drink off a little, too.

"There is something else going on though, Cord. I can feel it and smell it. We need to back the fuck off, starting right now."

"Don't worry, Ronnie. I think I've already been backed the fuck way off. That train has left the station."

"Yeah, you're probably right there."

"If she could play a card game like she plays the 'love ya, mean it' game, she'd be a rich woman. I had no idea. Never saw it. Never saw the bluff."

"Hey, that ain't exactly some run of the mill girl there, Cord." He nods at me. "There is definitely something she's got that very few have—and when she shines that particular light on you, well hey." He nods again and shrugs.

"Yeah," I say, "but you saw it, and her, for what it was. At the least, you knew something wasn't right and didn't like it."

"Cord, if she'da been purrin' on my lap and rubbing on my leg, I'd a gone after that like a dog on the first day of dove season. I'd have it much worse than you right now."

"Right, right. Sure you would have."

"I'm not bullshittin'. I would have followed her right out of here, just now, just like some whipped little boy. Cryin' for her to come back to me."

Ronnie has always been smarter than me, and I don't mind admitting that. He's playing this so well. He knows me, knows how to hit the right buttons, and I don't care because it still works on me. Ain't the first time this game has been played.

"Ego."

"What?"

"Pride."

"What game are we playing here, Ronnie?"

"Survivor."

"I give up—and I'm bored."

"All of that, all of those things are what saves you. That and a healthy dose of that certain uppity ass *you don't know who you're fuckin' messin' with*...thing." Ronnie stabbed his finger at me. He's grinning from ear to ear.

"So, wait a minute here. What're you now, a self-help therapist or something? A motivational coach?"

He looks down, then back up at me, "Hey, I can't have my meal ticket going south on me and turning into some head case that can't win at cards no more." He looks at me and smiles again.

"This has been a really fucked up Vegas trip." I reach out with my tumbler and wait for him to raise his. We clink and drink. I can really feel the booze now, and it seems to me that we probably need to get out of this deserted-ass suite and go back downstairs.

"Don't let that little bitch mess with your mind."

"What little bitch?"

"Seriously. I know it has to hurt. A little."

"Nah, this just confirms the fact that there is no one out there for me. Don't get me wrong, there's a bunch and I'll do my damnedest to work my way through the talent search. But... but, there is no *one* girl for me, pardner."

I slowly look at the finger I'm holding up for one and then look at him and bulge my eyes way out. He snorts, I laugh and slap him on the back.

"Fuck it. Let's get downstairs, Ronnie boy. We've gotta fly outta here tonight, but there's still time to cause trouble of some kind, ain't there? Break a heart or two?"

He shakes his head no. "We need to drink in your room or mine, where we can sleep where we fall. Sun coming up, public drunkenness, bar scene, cougars and young showgirls just getting off of work. None, absolutely none, of those are good things, sporty."

"Yeah, but I got to try and find Annie and say goodbye." I throw an arm over his shoulder. "C'mon, if we don't catch her in the lobby, we'll cab it over to the Riv."

"Cord."

"Ronnie."

We walk toward the suite door.

"Cord?"

I love throwing Ronnie curveballs.

The look he has on his face is priceless.

TWENTY-FIVE
Casey

If there's one thing that poker and baseball both have in common, it's that there is a time when you reach a point of no return. In baseball, it's when you commit to swing the bat or to steal a base. In poker, it's when you go all in on a hand. Either way, whether it was a good decision or a bad one doesn't matter anymore. You're committed.

I took one look at Mats, with his cocky, sadistic expression, and I drove my foot straight up into his crotch as hard as I could.

The blow landed with a solid *thwap*. Mats' eyes bulged. His knees bent, and he hunched over protectively, a small groan escaping his lips.

I didn't wait to see if he was going to fall on his own. I shouldered past him, giving him a good shove to the side as I passed. His wiry muscles were as hard as stone, but the guy still weighed a good thirty pounds less than me, and physics applies to assholes, too. He stumbled and collapsed, writhing and groaning on the ground.

Yeah, I was pretty committed at this point.

I race-walked through the casino, heading straight to security. When I got there, the kid on duty was eating Chinese food. He had a mouthful of noodles when he looked up at me and tried to swallow fast but choked instead.

I held up my hand. "Babe's expecting me."

He coughed into his hand, shaking his head. I ignored that and pushed open the door to Babe's office.

He was sitting at his desk, looking down at a pad of paper where he'd scrawled some numbers. When he saw me, his eye narrowed and he set down the pen. "Shawn didn't tell you I needed a few minutes?"

"If Shawn is your desk guy," I said, thumbing toward the door, "he's too busy choking on his General Tso's to tell anybody anything."

Babe nodded as if he already knew that. "Not a big deal." He looked me up and down. "You look flush, Casey. You run all the way down here?"

Ball buster to the end, huh? But I was done playing with this giant idiot. Him and all the rest. "Yeah," I said. "And I need my money. Now."

He turned up his hands. "Can't help you there, Case. Sorry."

A flash of panic went through me, followed quickly by anger. "What the hell are you talking about? I won. You've got the money. Now give it to me."

"You did win," Babe said, his voice calm and indulgent. "And it was mighty impressive, too. I wish it had been on TV. Damn, the way you called that final card?" He shook his head. "That's once in a lifetime shit right there."

"Where's my money?"

He cocked his head at me slightly. "You in a hurry or something?" He pointed at the seat in front of his desk. "Take a load off."

"No," I said. "I just want my money."

"I wasn't asking," Babe said, with a trace of a growl.

"I don't care," I snapped. "And yeah, I am in a hurry. So open up the safe and give me my goddamn money."

"Or what?" He stared at me.

I gave him the hardest glare I had. "I'm pushed over the line, Babe," I said in a low voice. "Either you give me my money, or I'm coming over that desk at you."

His eyebrows went up in surprise. "Wow. You're a tough guy now?"

"I'm not kidding."

"No, I believe you," he said, chuckling a little. "But the thing is..." He trailed off, opened a drawer, and pulled out a small pistol. The chuckling stopped, and his face became dark. "Thing is, that would be a big mistake."

I should have seen this coming. All of it. Not just the gun, but Babe welshing on the deal. I just didn't see how he could get away with it if he wanted to stay in Vegas. Word would get out that he couldn't be trusted. He'd be done. Was this haul enough for him to—

"Now sit down," he ordered.

"No," I said.

"The fuck you say?"

"I said no. If you're going to shoot me, do it."

His face hardened, and he leveled the pistol at my head. "Don't think I won't."

I stared back at him. "I don't doubt you would, under the right circumstances. But not here. Not in the security office of the Magnum Hotel on the Las Vegas strip. That might reinforce the idea that organized crime existed here. The Tourism Bureau might not like that."

He kept the gun pointed at me.

He was bluffing. Had to be.

I smiled. I actually fucking *smiled*. "And I know Lieutenant Nicky Raines would love to sink her teeth into that apple."

He regarded me for another moment, then slowly lowered the gun.

Bluff called.

Ride that wave.

"You're a fucking smartass, Casey," he said. "And everyone hates a smartass."

"Where's my money?"

Babe put the gun back into the drawer and pushed it shut.

"Gone."

"Gone?"

"I fucking stutter?"

"Where is it?"

He smiled at me then. A cruel, knowing smile. "I gave it to your little girlfriend."

"You gave it to—" I stopped, my mind whirring.

Was Cord right?

"What?" Babe said. "You didn't send her down here to get it?"

Shit.

He leaned forward on his elbows. "Because she said that you did. And it was obvious to everyone that the two of you were banging each other, so..." he shrugged. "So, I figured it was okay."

I swallowed.

It *was* okay. It had to be.

Babe kept smiling. "Unless...well, unless that little honey is fucking you over for the money. Is that it? Is that what's going on here?"

"It's fine," I said, but my voice sounded weak and distant.

Babe leaned back in his big leather chair and chuckled. It was the worst sound I'd ever heard.

"Sure it is, Case," he said around his laughter. "Sure it is."

TWENTY-SIX
Cord

It was meant to be. Another two minutes, or even if we had been looking the other way, and it would have been *poof*. Gone forever.

She's walking out of the Riv as we're walking in. Some poor old shit is having a hard time keeping up, rolling the silver luggage cart along behind her. She's walking about as fast as you can without it being a trot.

She's got some sexy sunglasses on, and her hair is tied back in a ponytail. The expensive white silk blouse, faded frayed jeans and heels make all the sense in the world. Just enough jewelry. Just, well, all-around hotness.

Even with the shades on, I can tell she sees me about the same time I see her as her head clicks over in our direction.

I veer to the left to block her way out.

"Oh, hey! Hey, babe! Our flight isn't until tonight? I'm all confused here."

Ronnie, who was lagging reluctantly behind anyway, walks over to the side about twenty feet away or so.

I stand there smiling, and with a little drunk shrug, I wink at her. "How 'bout some breakfast, lover?"

"Cord, get out of my way."

"But muffin, I don't understand." I put my hand on my heart. "Why oh why you want ta' treat me this a-way?"

The bellman lets go of the cart and comes up to me. He's about forty-five or so, under six foot, starting to gray at the edges. Nose has been broken before.

"Please, sir. Ms. Kozak is in a hurry." He's polite about it, but stern.

My guess? Broken-down boxer or maybe an ex-con. This is his daughter basically and even though I'm half drunk, I get it. I get the protective thing. With one like her, there are ten different ways to be hooked.

"No kidding?" I look around him and at her, "Where you headed, honey bunch?"

She looks down, nervously adjusts her sunglasses, and then glances over at Ronnie, maybe hoping he would usher me away.

Ronnie just stares back at us, leans on a pillar, and crosses his arms.

"Look here, sir," says the bellman. "We won't stand for any of this kind of thing here at the Riviera. No trouble."

"You'll have none, as long as you back off for a second, okay?"

The bellman stands his ground.

"Look, this ain't your business. I just need to say goodbye to this hot little slut. That's it. Seriously. Two minutes, pardner, and we're gone."

It took a second for what I said to actually sink in. He's probably still quick with a jab, I figure, but that's about it.

He takes a step in closer, and we're almost nose to nose. "You apologize to Ms. Kozak for what you just said."

I turn and laugh at her. "Annie, please do something here. Don't ruin who he thinks you are."

She smiles now and steps forward. "It's all right, Tom. I know him. He's obviously been drinking, but it's fine. If you can wait for me outside at the curb...and oh, maybe have them pull my car around?"

The bellman grins at her, taking the valet parking receipt and what looked like two twenties from her. Hell, he would have paid her.

He looks back at me, and the smile goes away. "All right, Ms. Kozak. I'll take care of everything."

He starts rolling the cart by me, toward the wall of doors. "You got your two minutes, asshole. After that, you're right, you will be gone. You just trust me on that."

"Okay, good. Great, Tom. Hey, thanks so much. Be careful with those bags now! They're worth a lot of money."

He gives me one more look over the shoulder and keeps rolling.

I turn back to her. "A *helluva* lot of money. Right, Annie?"

She just stares up at me and then takes her sunglasses off. Those green eyes are still beautiful, the body still perfect, the scent alluring as ever, but it just ain't the same. And that, when you get right down to it, is a very good thing.

"It's nothing to you, though, Cord. That's like an allowance or something. This was all a game for you, too. Life is a game to you."

"Well, it always was until you came along. No doubt about that. But I'll give you the credit you deserve, bitch. Only you have ever taken me for a real ride like that. Literally and figuratively."

She leaned in close and gave me a sexy smile, "So, besides that, cowboy, what do you want from me? How about, yes, I enjoyed having you. No, I don't love you. Yes, I used you like the tool you are. Anything else?"

"Thank you, darlin'."

She was still smiling at me, then blinked several times innocently. "Cord, that was all very mean of me to say. I'm sorry. I *really* am." Then she put a finger to her lips and, reaching up, touched mine.

"No, I mean it," I say. "As much as I mean anything, that is. Thank you. This is just what I needed. I needed to know for sure that you were really just a cheap little whore. Before you ran out of town, I mean."

It was her turn to laugh now, and she did. "Gotta go, *babe*.

'Kay?" She was all light and breezy now.

"Oh hey, wait. Somebody is looking for you, sweetheart. That mean ol' Casey. You know, the one who was threatening and scaring you so bad. He was confused at the Magnum after the game."

"Oh, he'll call me. He'll say he loves me. I'll tell him what he wants to hear, and he'll still think everything is going to be okay." She shakes her head. "Can you believe that? Then again, he's a different breed of dog than you are, stud boy."

"I bet there's been some other boys that you left barkin' and chasin' your car down the road, too, huh?"

"Like I said, gotta go, Cord. It's been fun."

I reach out softly and touch her elbow. "Wonder if breakin' hearts is the only thing you ever break? I mean, besides pointin' those cute little toes at the ceiling—which you are truly a professional at—I'll just wager you've got some illegal skills, too, girl."

"If I were you, I'd stop wagering. At least until you get to Atlantic City." She slides her sunglasses down, turns, and walks away.

"Have fun with that cash while it lasts, punkin'," I call after her. "Enjoy it, but you know as sure as I do, it won't last. There'll be a day, sooner than you think, when you wake up in that hot, stuffy, ol' double-wide trailer...again."

She just keeps going though, and I'll admit I watch her go while imagining that view with no faded jeans. She is some kind of sweet poison, no getting around that.

I follow her to the doors but stop short of going outside. I can feel Ronnie come up behind me, and we watch her walk up to the old bellman at the curb. He's standing next to the empty luggage rack.

Old Tom turns to look back at where we stand on the other side of the glass. He says something to her and jerks a thumb back at us. It makes me smile. She plays everybody and everything.

A red Miata, convertible of course, is sitting there waiting, and he hands her the keys. She smiles and says something. The old guy nods, points at the trunk, then nods again. They wave at each other, and she gets in, throwing her purse on the passenger seat. She pulls away from the curb and follows the long circular drive.

Gone.

"Hungry?" Ronnie asks.

"Kinda."

"Done drinking?"

"Not yet. Let's go back to Magnum." I nod outside. "Besides, Tommy out there is gonna kick my ass if we don't leave."

TWENTY-SEVEN
Casey

I got out of the Magnum as quick as I could. I thought about heading over to the Riviera, but that didn't seem like the right play somehow. I walked down the strip for a few minutes, thinking.

My mind and my gut argued back and forth for a solid ten minutes. The sun beat down on me, but I was used to it. I might as well be a Vegas native by now. Sweat trickled down my spine without cooling me.

Annie wasn't screwing me over. It didn't work that way. You don't step up to the plate and take the ball yard like I did in that suite only to have someone steal home plate while you're trotting around the bases. That's not how it works. Not in baseball, not in poker, not in life.

Sure, she might've played Cord, but he was an arrogant, famous son of a bitch who took her money and embarrassed her. And who's to say she even worked him, anyway? Or slept with him? All I had was him saying so, and he was still stinging from the final hand that cost him four hundred grand.

Men lie about all kinds of things. Especially where women and money are concerned.

But then why did she take all the money?

My money.

And where did she go?

I stopped at a payphone and stared at it.

What did I believe?

What was the truth?

What kind of cards was Annie playing? The ones she told me about, or something else entirely?

I reached for the phone receiver and was dialing before I even realized who I was calling. The phone rang twice while my heart pounded in my ears.

She picked up after the third ring. "Raines."

"Nicky," I said. "It's me."

She was silent for a moment. Then, "What the hell do you want?"

"I...I wanted to say I'm sorry. And—"

"Yeah, well, sorry was yesterday's news," Nicky said. "Today it's fuck you."

"Nicky, I need to talk to you. There's things I—"

"You said plenty already. Did plenty, too."

"Nicky, please."

"Don't give me that 'please' shit. What happened? Your little slut run out on you and now you need someone to bandage your bruised ego?"

"No," I said. "It's not that. It's just that—"

"Look, I'm busy here. I got something big going on. So, do me a favor, Casey, huh? Don't call me again."

"Wait. I—"

"As in ever," she said and broke the connection.

The click in my ear was followed by the dial tone. I pulled the receiver away and stared at it. My wounded finger throbbed, the first time I'd really noticed it since before the start of the big game with Cord. Carefully, I hung up the phone. I lowered my head until my forehead touched the plastic box. It was hot, and it burned, but not enough to pull away.

Why the hell did I call her? I knew she wouldn't help. She'd never choose me over her career. And me being with Annie, well, that sealed the deal.

Annie.
My queen of diamonds.
I pulled my head back from the phone.
Shit. I was so stupid.

"You should've called me first," Perry said. "I'da saved you the trip."

"You've seen her?"

He nodded. "Yeah. About half an hour ago."

"Was she alone?"

He squinted at me. "Alone?"

"Yeah, Perry," I said, impatient. "Alone. As in, not with anyone else."

He scowled. "Jeez, you're touchy."

"I'm in a hurry here."

"No shit."

"Perry."

"Okay, okay." He raised his hands to placate me. "Yeah, she was alone. It's just a strange question, is all. Who else would she be with, except you?"

Exactly.

"No one," I said, and I could hear the small bit of relief in my voice. "No one else."

Perry eyed me strangely. "You okay? You don't look right."

"I've been playing cards all night. Did she pick up her diamonds?"

He nodded. "Paid in full. With interest. In cash."

Of course, in cash, I thought.

"You sure you're okay?" Perry asked. "I've never seen you look so...so..."

"So fucked?"

"What?"

"I'm fucked," I said. "I decided to steal second, and the goddamn pitcher made a pickoff move. Now I'm in the pickle."

Perry nodded slowly, then shook his head. "Yeah, I don't get it. I mean, I get the baseball stuff, but..."

"I owe the Swede big," I told him. "She had the money, *my* money, to pay him off."

"Oh..." His expression grew sympathetic. "And she bought back the diamonds instead. I see."

"No, that's not it. There's still plenty left after that. There's enough for the diamonds, and the Swede, and for her and I to get away."

"So, you two are taking off?"

"Supposed to be. As soon as everything else is taken care of."

"Where'd you get the money?"

"Private game."

"You won it?"

"Yeah, I fucking won it. I beat Cord Needham."

Perry laughed at me then. I just stood and stared at him. With everything else that was happening, now I had to be mocked by a high-end pawnbroker?

He must've seen the look on my face, because he stopped laughing after a few seconds. "You're serious?"

"I don't have time for this. Did Annie say where she was going after here?"

He shook his head. "No."

"Did she leave me a message?"

"No. She didn't seem like she was in a big hurry, though." He paused, then said. "Then again, she was only here about ten minutes."

"How long ago did she leave?"

"Maybe half an hour ago, like I said. Could be twenty minutes, even." He shrugged. "Listen, did you really beat Needham? Because if you did, that is one hell of a cool story. I bet—"

I turned to leave.

"Casey?" he called after me.

I looked over my shoulder at him. "What?" I snapped.

"Did you call her?"

I froze. How could I be so stupid? "Not yet," I finally managed.

He shrugged. "I mean, if you guys had a plan, it sounds like it's going fine. She got the money and the diamonds, now she only needs you. Just call her."

I swallowed. He was right. It was the most obvious answer in the world. She was getting things in order, and I was the last thing. So why in the hell hadn't I thought to call her first thing?

"Can I use your phone?" I asked Perry.

"Sure," he said. "In my office."

I followed him. I took the battered white card with her initial A. on it out of my wallet and stared down at it. Perry handed me the phone, and I dialed. The line connected, and her phone rang. And rang. A cold dread tightened and coiled in my gut with every ring. The doubts I'd been pushing back frantically since the end of the poker game started to creep and slide past my defenses. Maybe Cord was right. Maybe Babe was right. Maybe she—

"Hello? Casey?"

Her voice in my ears paralyzed me for a moment. I felt that tightness in my stomach wash away.

"You there?" she asked.

I cleared my throat. "I'm here. Where are you?"

"I'm back at the Riviera, packing."

I remained silent for another few seconds. I could hear the sounds of traffic in the background. "I hear cars," I said.

"My windows open. I needed the fresh air after all that time in that card game. Listen, I thought you were going to meet me here."

Did we talk about that? I couldn't remember now. But it didn't matter. "I guess I forgot."

"You *forgot?*" She paused, then asked, "Are you having second thoughts, Casey?"

"No, I—"

"Because I don't want you to go unless you really want to. It has to be real for you, or it's no good for me."

"No, Annie, it's real. I want to go."

More than anything, that's what I want.

"Well, then get over here, baby. I'm almost ready to go."

"What about your diamonds?" I asked, testing her.

"I already picked them up."

I smiled. "What about the Swede?"

"Let's talk about that when you get here. Do you have to pay him? Can we just leave?"

"No," I said. "I have to pay. I don't want that debt following us around for the rest of our lives."

"You're right. That's smart."

We were quiet for a minute. Then I asked, "Why'd you leave so quick? After the game, I mean."

"Jesus," she said. "I was tired of how that cowboy asshole kept looking at me. Like I was a piece of meat. You couldn't tell?"

"Not really."

"Well, he was."

"What about the money, Annie? Why'd you take that? Why not just wait for me?"

She was silent for a few seconds. Then, in a hurt tone, she asked, "You don't trust me now? Is that it?"

"No," I said. "I do. I just don't understand."

"I got our money fast because I was afraid the cowboy or his manager or that security guy might not pay off. And I figured he'd give it to me easier than to you."

"Why?"

"You guys have some kind of macho thing going on. It would piss him off to give it to you. But I was your second, and I'm just some dumb girl, so he didn't have an issue with it."

I didn't answer right away, chewing my lip. I wished we were face-to-face so I could read her expression. All I had was her voice. Her beautiful voice.

"Casey?"

"I'm here."

"What does it matter how I got our money? I've got it, and we can get out of here."

She was right. And I believed her.

That's when I looked up through the office window and saw the Swede walk in through the front door.

TWENTY-EIGHT
Cord

The big plane lifts off gently and gains altitude quickly. I can't say leaving Vegas this time is anything but a damn relief. The lights fade quickly behind us as we head east.

Once we level off, Ronnie's seat goes back all the way before the little tone even sounds.

I'm bone tired, too, because we just kept drinking for a while today and then finally ate dinner at the Magnum early afternoon. Before we knew it, we were headed for the airport.

"You gonna sleep?"

No answer from Ronnie reclined next to me.

My problem is that even though we're in first class all the time now, I can't sleep on a plane. Bone tired or not, it won't be happening. Period. Ronnie is the exact opposite.

I look out the dark window at nothing, and my mind is pretty much blank, too.

"Would you like anything right now?" The flight attendant snuck up on me. She could be my mother, if my mother was still alive. They just keep getting older and older.

"No ma'am."

She looks at Ronnie and sees he's out cold already.

"Actually, how 'bout a Bloody Mary? Please."

She gets another few drink orders and then goes behind the partition to make them.

"Can't sleep."

His voice makes me jump. "Jesus, son, you scared the livin' shit outta me."

"Been awake the whole time."

"This is some kind of record, a damn first for you. You're usually snorin' before the wheels are up. What the hell's wrong? You must be sick."

He doesn't move, and he doesn't open his eyes.

"Ronnie?"

The attendant arrives with a tray.

"Here we go."

"Well, thank you, ma'am."

She spreads out a little cloth napkin and sits my Bloody Mary down on the tray.

"I brought you something to snack on, too, hon'." She smiles at me and sets down a bowl of warmed, assorted nuts. "If you do get hungry, you let me know now. I'll be back."

Ronnie holds a finger up, "Ma'am, could I possibly get what he's drinking there?"

"Why, sure. Be right back."

Ronnie leaves his seat reclined, but he sits up a little straighter and turns his head to look at me.

The attendant glides away, and I grab a handful of the nuts.

"So, Ronnie, like I said, you should be comatose right now. What's up?" I pick out two cashews and pop them in my mouth.

"Gotta talk to you, man." His voice is low and serious.

I stare at him for a second, trying to decide what this is. "Okay, shoot." I keep my voice down, too.

There are only dim lights on in first class and it's pretty quiet. A few people reading but a lot are sleeping already.

"I was gonna wait until we landed but that just ain't right, and I can't hold this in, anyway. You need to know."

"Is this the Aruba thing? Shit! I knew..."

"No, Cord."

Ronnie's eyes go to the front, and he smiles at the attendant as she brings his drink. He nods at her and off she goes again. Stirring his drink around with the celery, Ronnie is frowning and deep in thought.

I don't say anything smart-ass, or hurry him. This is one of those times. Like a 2:00 a.m. phone call. It ain't gonna be good.

"When we boarded, and you hit the head right away? Well, I got a quick call while you were in there. Real quick. It was Jill Bookman."

"Laura's sister?" Ronnie had actually dated her back in the day. Laura introduced them to each other.

"Yup."

"No kidding? Hey, she was always a good girl. We get home, we should all do something like the old days."

Ronnie just looked at me with a blank stare.

"What? Is she married or something?"

"She said your phone had been off for the last two hours. She didn't want to leave a message."

"Well...oh, man. Oh, shit. I haven't called Laura for like four damn days, what with everything going on." Whether I meant cards or Annie, I wasn't sure. "What'd she say?"

"Cord..."

"She's leaving me for good, right? Won't be there when we get back from A.C.? All my shit will be in the front yard. Can't say as I blame her."

"Cord, she...she's dead. Laura's dead."

I just stare at him, because well, that can't be right. No, no, that can't be right at all.

"But...wait. What...no, no...Laura's waiting...she's in... Laura is...bad mistake." I can't put the right words together.

Ronnie reached over and put his hand on my forearm. "It was a car wreck. On I-35, right at the merge with I-10. No one else in the car, she ran off the highway in a pouring rainstorm. They pronounced her dead at the scene."

I think I'm smiling at him. Trying to push this off, dodge it, like everything else in my life. "Ronnie, this is a huge mistake, man." I feel two big ol' tears, one on each side, racing each other down to my chin. "No way." My smile quivers.

"No, it's true, buddy. It's true, pardner. God, I'm sorry, Cord. Really." He squeezes my arm, and I put my other hand on top his.

"Ronnie, besides you, she knew me longer than anybody."

"I know."

"No, I mean *really* knew me. Like you."

"Yessir."

The attendant comes by, pauses, and her expression changes to concern. Ronnie puts up his hand and shakes his head no to her.

"She loved me. Loved my worthless ass."

Ronnie pats my arm. "She did that."

The jet's engines muffled sound is the only sound for a long minute.

"I loved her, too, Ronnie. I know I didn't show it, and I shoulda married her...I loved her. Dammit."

"I know you did."

"I did."

I knew as soon as I said that, it was wrong. If I'd married Laura, that would have killed her too, just in another way. Slower and more painful.

We don't say anything more for a long while.

Ronnie finally gets up to go hit the restroom.

It's about a five-hour flight anyway, but I think before this over it'll be the longest flight I've ever been on.

In a daze, I slowly turn to the window. I see a weak reflection of my face framed by the unending darkness of the night out there.

I move closer to the window just so darkness is all I see.

TWENTY-NINE
Casey

"Shit," I said as the Swede was followed by Mats and another guy about twice his size. "They're here."

"Who's there, baby?" Annie asked in my ear.

"The Swede. He's here."

"Where are you?"

"Perry's. The pawn shop."

"What are you doing *there*?" she asked.

"I—"

"Never mind. It doesn't matter. Can you get out?"

I looked over at Perry, whose eyes were as big as roulette wheels. "Is there a back way out of here?"

He nodded and pointed a shaking finger behind me. I turned to look. There was a fire door.

"I think I can get out," I told Annie. "I'll call you when I—"

The shotgun blast was loud and made me jump in surprise. The doorknob to Perry's office exploded from the door at the same time and flew into the opposite wall, leaving nothing in the door but splintered wood around a jagged hole.

The big guy kicked the door open and strode in, a sawed-off pump shotgun in his hands. He leveled it at both of us, smoke curling from the barrel.

"Oh my God," Perry whimpered.

"What was that?" Annie asked me. "Are you okay?"

Mats followed him into the room then stepped aside for the Swede.

"I'm not going anywhere," I told her.

The Swede came into the office. He glanced at Perry, the office surroundings, then at me. "Hello, Mr. Brunnell," he said.

I swallowed and didn't reply.

"Stay there," Annie said. "I'll bring the money to you."

"Okay," I croaked.

"I'll be there in half an hour."

I nodded, even though she couldn't see me. "I love you," I told her.

She broke the connection.

Mats stepped across the office and snatched the phone from my hand. He slammed the receiver down on the desk, grabbed me by the front of my shirt, and pushed me into a chair. Then he leaned in close. "I'm going to enjoy this," he snarled. "Paybacks are a motherfucker, *pojke*."

The Swede cleared his throat, and Mats reluctantly pulled away from me. Everyone in the room turned their attention to the Swede. He pulled a chair from a small desk against the wall and put it in the center of the room. He sat down and crossed his legs, European style.

"So, Mr. Brunnell. It appears our business is at an end."

"I've got your money," I said.

My finger throbbed.

"I've heard differently," he replied.

"I do. I took it off of Cord Needham. In a private game."

The Swede smiled. "Yes, I've heard that as well. I have to admit, I was surprised. I didn't think you had it in you to win the kind of money you owed me from anyone at all, much less a professional like Mr. Needham. In fact, I had it as long odds that you would even find some weak whale to win it from."

"I beat him."

"Yes, I know. As I said, I am aware of your game and your victory. It is something to be proud of, that is for certain. Players of Cord Needham's caliber are difficult to beat, even for other professionals."

"I have your money," I said.

He cocked an eyebrow. "Do you? Very well, then. Pay me, and we'll all be on our way."

"It's not here."

He gave me a thin smile. "Of course, it isn't."

"But it's on the way," I assured him. "She's bringing it."

"She?"

"Annie."

"Ah." He nodded slowly. "And when will she be here?"

"Soon." I glanced at Mats and the gorilla with the shotgun. "Very soon."

The Swede pursed his lips. "Can you be more specific, Mr. Brunnell? Because, to be perfectly blunt, I've lost my patience with you."

I pointed at the phone. "That was her on the phone. She said she was coming."

"How long?"

"Half an hour," I said, and licked my lips. "She said it would take half an hour."

The Swede nodded, taking a deep breath and letting out in a long exhale. Then he said, "I'll tell you what, Mr. Brunnell. I will show you this last bit of patience. This last bit of grace. I will wait for one hour. Just so there's no mistake. One full hour. How would that be?"

"An hour is fine," I said. "She'll be here before that. She has the money."

"Oh, I know she has the money," the Swede answered.

Parcella must have called him, I realized.

"That's not really the question, is it?" he said. "The question is, will she bring the money here?"

I looked around the room. Perry was staring at the Swede in terror. He must've figured out that his fate was sealed to mine now. If Annie brought the money, everything would go back to the way it was, minus a new office door. If she didn't, he was going to join me in a hole in the desert.

If.

There was no if.

She would come.

The Swede gave me a placid look, then glanced at his watch. "An hour," he said, "and then we'll settle your account, one way or the other."

I nodded. "I understand. But she's bringing the money."

Mats shook his head at me. "You stupid fuck, Casey. That bitch isn't coming. And when she doesn't show, I'm going to take you apart, piece by piece. I'm going to—"

"How's your balls, Mats?" I asked him.

He clenched his jaw, then pointed at me. "You'll pay for that, too. Don't you worry, *pojke*." He glanced at his watch. "In about fifty-nine minutes, you'll pay."

I forced myself to smile at him. "We'll see."

"Yes, we fucking will," he agreed.

I leaned back in the chair and tried to relax. My heart was thumping like a bass drum in my chest, but I didn't want to show them. An hour was plenty of time. More than enough. Annie would show up with time to spare. We'd pay off and get the hell out of Vegas for good.

She'll come.

She has to.

She'll come.

I know it.

My heart was racing, and I swallowed past the lump in my throat.

"She'll be here," I whispered, more to myself than anyone else. "She's coming."

She will come.

She will.

I know she will.

Mats stared. The gorilla with the shotgun stood. The Swede sat. Perry whimpered.

We waited.

THIRTY
Babe

Babe Parcella cruised into Spring Valley, a suburb just southwest of the strip, headed toward his new condo. It's damn nice. Expensive and somewhat exclusive, but not too flashy. Just right, really. He's been upgrading lately, that's for sure. What he won't do, though, is be a dumbass about it.

Like this car he was driving right now. A brand new Cadillac CTS, mocha metallic color. Loaded inside and high ticket, for sure, but no bling rims or any of that shit. The best damn luxury car there ever was, in his opinion. He'd always drove them, even when he couldn't afford it.

Babe liked the public perception of himself he had created here in Vegas. Just some big bear stomping around that looked badass and took care of security for a casino. Not the sharpest tack either, but scary and dangerous if you fucked with him.

What people didn't know about him was that he actually was a sharp tack. He enjoyed the arts, expensive wines, antiques, gourmet cooking, and in general, the finer things in life. Trouble is, that all takes money. So, he took money. Whenever, and wherever, he could. Parcella had a number of different scams going on right then, and they all contributed to the whole.

Yeah, it was far more work to manage and monitor, but it was better this way. Better than just one big gig. With one major operation, it's too open, too glaring. When whatever that big thing is comes falling down, a guy can get left with nothing but his dick in his hand afterwards.

All scams, big or small, eventually fall apart or dry up sooner or later. Like anything else, they all have a lifespan. That's just the way it is. That's why Babe always had other things going on and others lined up, waiting to happen.

He glided slowly around a corner a couple of blocks away from his place. The manicured properties slid by, and the lawn sprinklers that made every blade of grass possible were in full morning mode. It was mid-morning, and he was beat to shit. That card game last night had gone on for fucking ever. Yesterday, he decided to take a few days off and man, did he ever need it.

As he cruised along, his active mind examined where he was at with all this recent bullshit. And to be sure, there had been a lot of bullshit. Some of it good, some of it worthless, and some just good to remember.

Casey? Well, he was sorry to see him go, actually. Sorry, because he wasn't really that bad a guy, but also sorry because he'd always been a steady little moneymaker and contributor to the Babe Parcella Charity Retirement Fund. He finally had to go, though, and it was really as simple as that. He was like a sacrifice fly. Batter's out, but the runners advance.

The Swede and him were on better terms than ever before. The relationship was mutually beneficial as they both regularly made decent money in the underbelly world of gambling. The Swede had also appreciated the call from him earlier this morning, pointing him to Casey. He would no doubt give Babe a little cash kiss for that.

Annie Kozak. Now there, there was one to remember. For many reasons. The pure and blinding attraction she could cause was a biggie with her. The sex just dripped off her, and that's what made it all run. In his time, he had bedded more girls and women than he could count. Most were beautiful, too, so good looking that if he didn't have his job title and or something to hold over them, they wouldn't even sneeze in his direction. None of them though, not one, could match her sexy little self. She was one in a million, if not one of a kind.

It was a no go trying to shake that little bitch down. She was way ahead of you, too far out in front of the game. The best he had been able to do with her was finagle a little payoff when he opened his safe this morning and handed her Casey's winnings. She knew that he knew what was going on and what she was up to. So, Annie had done the smart thing and paid off.

Cord Needham and Ronnie Turnbull were still in play, though. They had some great potential. Maybe it could last a while, too. Cord's loyal pit bull manager thought that he had really kicked Babe's ass. Really put him in his place and shoved him back out the door. But Turnbull had a surprise waiting for him. In about a month or so, maybe two, Babe would call him and say that someone else had called him about the Aruba thing. Maybe that caller was even a private investigator or something.

"I mean, damn Ronnie, there must be something to this thing. I don't want to know the details, but what can I do to help? I can probably arrange for convincing this P.I. guy to shut the hell up, but it'll cost." He could hear that future conversation, and it made him grin.

Babe made a left onto his street, Miners Court. He rubbed his neck, trying to work out the kinks, and sighed heavily.

Finally, there was always the security business in general, which had a hundred different little money legs to it. Cash would continue to trickle in, just as he preferred. Nothing to attract any attention, not too much in any one area, just a steady and constant stream.

At last, he pulled into his driveway but also saw his neighbor one building over, just getting into his car. Terry Lister was an okay guy, nice enough for a civilian, but he was such a boring asshole and an idiot on top of that. Babe always tried to just wave, or if a conversation was unavoidable, he kept it short.

Across the way, Terry had his hand on the car door, smiling and waving. Babe waved back and muttered to himself. "Please, just get in and drive away...please."

For a minute, he pretended to be gathering stuff together and looking in his business bag for make-believe things. He looked out of the corner of his eye, and his neighbor was still standing by his car, grinning and waiting.

Babe heaved another heavy sigh. *Shit...I'm too tired to deal with this goofy asshole...*

"Hey, Babe!" Cheery and loud.

"Hey, Terry." Babe reached back in the car like he's forgotten something. *Just go. GO, you ass.*

"How's things, big guy?"

"Not bad, Terry, not..." Mid-sentence, he looked down, went to his belt with his left hand and held up a finger to his neighbor with his right hand.

"Babe Parcella," he said, answering the dead air.

It worked. Terry nodded at him, waved again, and got into his car and backed out of the driveway. Before pulling away for good, though, he waved again.

Babe all but skipped and whistled to his front door. He walked into his cool house and immediately felt better. Straightening a painting that was already perfectly hung in the foyer, he strode down a wide hallway and into a large gourmet kitchen. This sparkling, gleaming room was probably his favorite space in the house. It had all the latest in appliances, dark cherry cabinetry, imported slate flooring, recessed lighting, and a large prep island. On the other side of the polished granite bar, it also had Benjamin Lock sitting on one of the padded barstools.

"Babe." A voice like heavy gravel. He grinned, nodded his head coolly, and shifted his six foot four frame around a little.

Babe couldn't find any words yet. He just stared back at the big man.

Lock fished out a cigarette and lit up. He held up a glass of wine. "Nice, *really nice*, place you got here."

"Bennie boy, to what do I owe this little visit? Whatcha got for me?" Babe had decided how to try and play this. It had been all he could do not to piss his pants when he'd seen Lock just sitting there. It had been probably been ten years since he'd been sent up. Ben Lock was not somebody to fuck with. At all. In fact, you just didn't have a choice. He fucked with you. And he usually meant death.

Babe casually made his way to the right cupboard. "Mind if I join you?"

"Too late, Babe. I just stumbled onto it when I got my glass." He held up Babe's Sig, set it down on the counter next to his wine glass, and shrugged. "Pure luck."

Babe saw now that Lock was wearing surgical gloves. The man's other hand was still under the raised counter.

"Who's got you doing this, Bennie?"

"I've never liked Bennie." He looked at Babe and cocked his head to the side. "I like Benjamin or even just Ben."

"Whatever they're paying you, I'll pay double."

"It ain't all about money, Babe."

"What's it about, then?"

He shrugged. "You're too good at what you do. You are too successful. Isn't that weird?"

"Who? Tell me."

"Right now, the weight of the world is about to come crashing down around you. And you don't even know it." He finished his wine and set it down gently. "Damn, that's good wine. Anyway, though, I'm talking raids, search warrants, and on and on."

"What are you talking about?"

Lock raised his eyebrows. "Nicky Raines, of course. The guy who pays me has a very good contact downtown. Raines is at the casino right now, as we speak. In your office. With search warrants and federal agents and all that shit."

Babe shook his head slightly. "No way."

"It's true," Lock said. "I'm sure they'll be here in an hour or so. Then she'll have your head on a plate. Which means others, too. And that can't happen."

Babe shook his head again. "No...I...there's more time. This place isn't in my name. It's—"

"In your mother's name? Like the cops haven't figured out that little gangster trick?"

"My...grandmother's name," Babe said, ending weakly. His heart had started to pound the moment he saw Lock, but now it kicked into overdrive.

"Nice variation," Lock said. "So, I give you maybe two hours before they figure it out. If they haven't already. I mean, there could be a SWAT van in the driveway right now. So we don't have much time here."

"I'll lam it," Babe said. "You won't see me here again."

Lock shook his head sadly and brought his Ruger up from below the counter. It had the long suppressor Babe expected. "The Swede is just saving you from all of that pain and mental anguish."

"Bennie, please...c'mon." Babe leaned toward the arch that led to the hallway.

"Don't make me chase your fat ass and put about six in you. We can do this with one." Lock raised the gun and said, "Also, what the hell did I *just* tell you about calling me Bennie?"

Babe ran anyway, but in the end, it didn't really matter.

JIM WILSKY is a crime fiction writer. His first solo novel, titled *Cargo*, is nearing completion. In addition, he has published a short story collection, *Sort 'Em Out Later*. To that end, over fifty of his short stories have been published in some of the most respected online magazines such as *Shotgun Honey*, *Beat To A Pulp*, *All Due Respect*, *Yellow Mama*, *Flash Bang Mysteries*, *A Twist of Noir* and many others. He has also contributed stories to several anthologies, including *A Grifter's Song*, *Kwik Krimes*, *Both Barrels* and *The Odds Are Against Us*.

Jim resides in Texas. You can keep up with Jim at TrippingTheTrigger.blogspot.com.

FRANK ZAFIRO was a police officer in Spokane, Washington, from 1993 to 2013. He retired as a captain. He is the author of numerous crime novels, including the River City novels, Stefan Kopriva mysteries, the Charlie-316 series with Colin Conway, Bricks & Cam Jobs with Eric Beetner, and more.

Frank lives in Redmond, Oregon, with his wife Kristi, dog Richie, and a very self-assured cat named Pasta. He is an avid hockey fan and a tortured guitarist.

You can keep up with him at FrankZafiro.com.